CECELIA'S SIN

Cecelia's Sin

a novella by

WILL D. CAMPBELL

with a Historical Introduction by

ERIC W. GRITSCH

MERCER UNIVERSITY PRESS • MACON, GEORGIA 31207

ISBN 0-86554-213-9

Printed in the United States of America
Second printing, December 1985
Third printing, November 1993

The paper used in this publication meets the minimum requirements
of American National Standard for Information Sciences—
Permanence of Paper for Printed Library Materials, ANSI Z39.48–1984.

Library of Congress Cataloging-in-Publication Data

Campbell, Will D.
Cecelia's sin.

Includes bibliographical references.
1. Geronymus, Cecelia.
2. Anabaptists—Netherlands—Biography.
3. Anabaptists. I. Title.
BX4946.G47C35 1983 284'.3'0924 {B} 83-819

ISBN 0-86554-213-9 (perfectbound)

Table of Contents

Dedication

For
Penny, Bonnie, and Webb,
heirs of Cecelia

Preface

THE WRITER OF fiction can create characters, assign roles, plot a course. But he dare not expect his people always to do what they are told. Those he claims as his own can become quite devious, going in unexpected directions, sometimes usurping the authority of their creator—in short, behaving much the same as real people do. I had heard such talk from others long before I decided to write a novel. When I was working on *The Glad River* it happened to me. Halfway through the book my principal character, Doops Momber, began writing a story of his own.

I was telling the story of three young men who lived during the middle of the twentieth century. His was a tale of a woman and two men who lived four hundred years earlier.

I had an inbred acquaintance with those of whom I wrote. Doops and Kingston Smylie were from Mississippi—my home. Fordache "Model T" Arceneau lived in Louisiana. I had lived there too. Doops's characters, Cecelia Geronymus, Pieter Boens, and Goris Cooman, lived in Amsterdam, a city I had never visited, and in a time of which I knew little. Did the character know something his creator did not?

Why was he doing this to me? I had given him name, being, and purpose. Why could he not be content to let me tell of his adventures? I was the potter. Or so I had assumed. He did not seem so ready to accept the role of clay. He was getting in my way, and at a time when I was feeling the pressure of a publisher's deadline.

I resented his trespass and at first tried to dissuade him, but when he stopped writing as quickly as he had begun, he left me with an added frustration. I had begun to learn things from him and to understand what he was up to. For example, I had named him Doops without knowing where the word came from. During the period of his intrusion I learned that *Doopsgesinde* was a Dutch word which meant "baptism minded," or "water minded," and was the term the Anabaptists, the people of whom he wrote, sometimes used when referring to themselves. Could it be that he had taken his name from this strange group? Had he somehow descended from them and was trying to tell me that I had as well? Instead of my having chosen a name for my central character, had it been given to me by the character himself?

Doops? *Doopsgesinde.* If what I had chosen to call him was merely a coincidence, it was an interesting one.

And the same with Fordache Arceneau. I discovered that "fordache" was an Indian word, appropriated by the Cajuns, and meant "one under severe penalty, destined to much suffering." I had not known what an apt beginning I had given to one who was supposed to have had little more than a walk-on part but whose imprisonment and death made him pivotal to the telling of the tale.

When Doops quit writing, rejoined his friends, and put me in charge of the novel once more, I had become foolishly infatuated with Cecelia Geronymus, plagued by adolescent fantasies. At the end of his brief profile Doops let her be drowned in a sack in the Amstel River, leaving me with my fancy and a minimum of information about her. What were her early years like? Who were her kin? Were there flaws in this beautiful person he had sketched? Had a romance developed between her and one of the others during the long winter months when she was alone with them in that upstairs room? If so, which one? Certainly I had the right to know of whom to be jealous.

He left me with none of the answers. Just a curious longing to know more of a woman I deeply respected and admired.

When Fordache died, under conditions similar to the death of Cecelia, Doops had some free time. I tried to persuade him to complete the story he had abandoned. He politely declined, pursued his own career and, I heard, became involved in the Civil Rights Movement and is writing a book about it. Convinced that he would write no more of Cecelia I resolved to do it myself, filling in the blanks, expanding, trying to answer my questions about her and the cause for which she was willing to die. (I am grateful to Holt, Rinehart, and Winston for the use of Doops's material which appeared in *The Glad River*.) Perhaps I cannot complete her story as well as he began it, yet he has left me no choice but to try.

More important than the origin of words was something else I gained from Doops's unfinished story. I came to have a strong suspicion that there exists a nexus between the Baptists of Doops's time and place and the gentle but tough little band of left-wingers known as Anabaptists, or *Doopsgesinde*. (I am indebted to Professor Gritsch and his historical introduction to this volume for confirming that the suspicion was justified.) Despite my suspicion and his historical support, however, I find little similarity.

In the first place, few of Doops's Baptists, and even fewer of ours four decades later, would look with much favor on the notion of being related to "left-wingers." Cecelia's community was communal. Doops's kin held to the tenet of private property with fierce purpose.

Her people were committed pacifists. Those of Doops's day were the first to go away to fight the nation's wars. She believed in the total separation of Church and State and expected no quarter from the political sector. Doops's Baptists have heard the siren song of Caesar, fly his flag alongside the banner of Christ, and will haul him into his own court to exact special privilege.

The Anabaptists would not take an oath, would not serve on juries, and would not have been allowed to do so because they so unfeignedly opposed the death penalty. At the trial of Doops's friend, the Baptist prosecutor impaneled an all male and all Baptist jury who, in the name of Jesus, sent Fordache to the electric chair.

Because positions of prominence were arrived at by torture and execution, Cecelia was unacquainted with sexual inequality. Women were as willing, and as apt, to achieve leadership roles through martyrdom as men. Top leadership among Baptist women in the latter years is to be found only in their own auxiliary groupings.

Not even the mode of baptism survived the years. Cecelia and her friends were fugitives on the run, hunted like rabbits by armed horsemen. They baptized each other in secret by pouring water from a dipper or sprinkling from a saucer in someone's attic. Doops's Baptists, popular and secure, announce the ritual in paid ads in the morning newspaper and insist that it be by complete immersion in an electrically heated tub. The dissimilarity is shattering to the notion of kinship. Yet the historical nexus cannot be denied and can be seen clearly in the Amish, the Mennonites, and others. But Doops's folk were Baptists.

Because her cause failed where they were concerned, some would say that Cecelia died in vain. I believe she would say, with many past and present, that an act of faithfulness is our only vocation.

For that Doops would embrace her as Sister.

Will D. Campbell
Mt. Juliet TN
Winter 1983

Acknowledgments

THE AUTHOR IS indebted to *Martyrs Mirror*, a book which chronicles the persecution of dissident Christians from the time of Christ to 1660, the year of its publication, for the use of certain names, places, dates, and some exposure to the vernacular. Although this is a work of fiction, a few specific incidents are based on historical events recorded in *Martyrs Mirror.* The book was edited by Thielman J. van Braght and translated from the Dutch by Joseph F. Sohm. It is published in the United States by Herald Press, Scottdale, Pennsylvania.

Birth of the Baptist Movement

by Eric W. Gritsch

MARTIN LUTHER CALLED them *Schwärmer*—radicals who swarm about like bees on the loose. Governments hunted them as "Anabaptists"—rebaptizers (from the Greek *anabaptizein*) who violated the laws of imperial Christendom by practicing a second baptism.[1] They were also known as "communitarians" because some of them lived in communes and shunned private property. Historians termed them "Swiss Brethren" or their own name for themselves, "Brethren in Christ."

They appeared first in Zurich, Switzerland, in the 1520s, after Ulrich Zwingli, the leader of the Swiss German reform movement, became the chief religious spokesman for the city. Starting out as one of Luther's adherents, Zwingli had persuaded the city fathers to abolish Roman Catholicism in favor of a much simpler Christian way of life patterned after early Christian principles as evidenced in the

---

[1]Protestant reformers like Luther's friend Philip Melanchthon urged political authorities to apply the ancient imperial laws against heretics. These laws called for the death penalty. See John S. Oyer, *Lutheran Reformers Against Anabaptists* (The Hague: Nijhoff, 1964), p. 174.

New Testament. A cadre of young men urged Zwingli to move as fast as possible to establish a community which would restitute these first Christian ways: catechetical instruction, followed by baptism after a personal confession of faith; prayer and Bible study groups, which would search for proper clues to arrange communal life; a simple Lord's Supper instead of the pompous medieval Roman Mass which would embody the fellowship of believers; and a commitment to Christian witness in the world which would reject any alliance with political government. Conrad Grebel, a young scholar trained in the humanities and in religion, and his friend Feliz Manz, both of whom were sons of influential families in town, urged Zwingli to adopt a religious platform which would establish a church free of governmental interference.

Zwingli and the city council held a public Christian disputation to determine what should be done. Zwingli himself favored a gradual transition from Roman Catholicism to a public Christian life based on the Bible. He contended that ancient traditions like infant baptism and close ties between church and state should not be discarded. Grebel and his group disagreed. They contended that it was the fusion of the Christian faith with political powers since Emperor Constantine I (306-337) which had brought about the perversions in medieval Christendom. Infant baptism had become much more an initiation into obedient citizenship than a sign of membership in the body of Christ. Did not religious wars, superstition, and other evils stem from the unfortunate alliance between church and state? Grebel and his group argued that the time for compromise had passed and that Christians must recover the stance of New Testament Christianity with its mandate to witness in the world without becoming identified with it.

When the public disputations disclosed opposition to the views of Grebel and his supporters, the "brethren" began to hold meetings in their homes, affirming their commitment to restituting what they called biblical Christianity rather than compromising. On 21 January 1525, the Zurich Council decreed that such meetings were illegal and that infant baptism would be retained in accordance with imperial law. Violaters would be prosecuted, and, if found guilty, would be banned from the city, imprisoned, or indeed executed if necessary. Grebel and his supporters refused to obey. On the evening of the day that the Council issued its decree, they held a meeting and, after prayer, Grebel baptized George Blaurock (so called because he wore a blue coat), a former Catholic priest, who in turn baptized all the others present. Other "second baptisms" soon followed in the city and countryside. An Anabaptist movement had been born, subject to criminal prosecution.[2]

Since the "brethren" held meetings which included adult baptisms and simple Lord's Suppers almost every day of the week despite their prohibition, the Zurich Council had Feliz Manz and twenty others arrested and thrown into the "witch tower" (Hexenturm). Aided by friends, thirteen men and seven women escaped within days. Manz went into the countryside where he continued to rebaptize and hold meetings. Grebel had escaped arrest earlier by doing the same thing. Both Manz and Blaurock were apprehended in 1526 and sentenced to life imprisonment, after it had become clear during a hearing conducted by Zwingli, that they would not recant their views. Two weeks after their sentencing, they escaped again, but Manz was recaptured in December 1526. The authorities condemned him to death by drowning in Lake Zurich, a mode of punishment reserved for women convicted of witchcraft. His death on 5 January 1527 made him the first martyr of the movement. Grebel had been struck down by the plague in the summer of the previous year.

The Anabaptist movement nevertheless continued to grow. A South German convert to the movement, Michael Sattler, became the new leader of the Swiss brethren and on 27 February 1527 he assembled all those who could manage to come in Schleitheim, near Schaffhausen, Switzerland. He requested everyone to adhere to a confession of faith he had written, entitled "Brotherly Union of a

[2]The historical details of Anabaptist origins in Zurich are in Fritz Blanke, *Brothers In Christ*, tr. Joseph Nordenhaug (Scottdale PA: Herald Press, 1964).

Number of Children of God Concerning the Seven Articles." These seven "articles" mandated that: (1) adult believers' baptism takes the place of infant baptism; (2) violators of the confession be banned from the community in accordance with early Christian practice (Matt.18:15-20); (3) the Lord's Supper be celebrated as a simple meal to symbolize unity in discipleship; (4) the community be separated from the political world, be it government and/or state church; (5) there be pastors to function as "shepherds" whose financial and other support be supplied solely by the members; (6) the community practices non-resistance and pacifism; and (7) no oaths be sworn because Christ forbade them (Matt. 5:34).[3] Many of those who signed the Schleitheim confession were later martyred. Sattler was burned at the stake on 27 May 1527; his wife was drowned a few days later. Blaurock was caught by Austrian authorities in Tyrol and burned at the stake on 6 September 1529.

Martyrdom only spurred the Anabaptist movement to greater efforts. Jacob Huter, another Austrian from Tyrol, created a communitarian group known as Huterites in the 1530s. This community was committed to living according to the biblical injunction of sharing worldly goods and shunning private property (Acts 4:34-35). To escape persecution, the Huterites moved to Moravia (southeastern Czechoslovakia) where they founded communes known as "brethren farms" (*Brüderhof*). Huter himself was arrested and burned at the stake in Innsbruck in 1536, but his communes lived on in Czechoslovakia, Hungary, Rumania, Russia, and, since 1874, in North America (Montana, South Dakota, Canada). Some Huterites went to South America (Paraguay). Their identification of private property with sin, their view of history as a struggle between Christianity and power politics, and their dedication to a simple agricultural life have made them the subject of fascinating sociological studies.[4]

---

[3]See John C. Wenger, "The Schleitheim Confession of Faith, Translated Into English, . . ." *The Mennonite Quarterly Review* 19 (1945): 243-53.

[4]See John A. Hostetler, *Huterite Society* (Baltimore: Johns Hopkins Univer-

Some leaders survived because their vocational skills were deemed more valuable to society than their religious convictions. Pilgram Marbeck, another Tyrolian Anabaptist, found a haven in Strassbourg, where he constructed a complex system of waterworks utilizing various small rivers. The Protestant establishment of the city tried to persuade him to give up his opposition to infant baptism and his commitment to a separatist church free of government involvement, but Marbeck persisted in his views. He was asked to leave the city but was given time to sell his house. Since the city of Augsburg had called him to take charge of its water and sewer systems, he settled there and died a natural death in 1536. The city fathers kept him employed although he steadfastly maintained his views despite many warnings to change them.[5]

The principal reformers of the sixteenth century, including Martin Luther, John Calvin, and Martin Bucer, linked the Swiss Anabaptists with other dissenting groups which they regarded as seditious. Luther, in particular, propagated the notion that all Anabaptists were followers of Thomas Müntzer, a Saxon Lutheran pastor who had become involved in the peasant rebellion of 1525. Müntzer had envisaged a kingdom of God on earth created by force and violence if peaceful means should prove unsuccessful. He had demanded the abolition of all externals, be they sacraments or anything else related to the institutional church. After the defeat of the peasants in May 1525, Müntzer was caught and beheaded as a seditious rebel. Luther saw his satanic spirit embodied in the Anabaptist movement which, he contended, must be eradicated by force. Yet the first Swiss Anabaptists had made it clear that Müntzer's methods violated their commitment to nonresistance and pacifism.[6]

---

sity Press, 1974). Also Robert Friedmann, *Hutterite Studies. Essays*, ed. Harold S. Bender (Goshen: Mennonite Historical Society, 1961).

[5]On his life and work see William and Walter Klaassen, eds. and trs., *The Writings of Pilgram Marbeck* (Scottdale PA: Herald Press, 1978).

[6]See the letter of Conrad Grebel to Müntzer, dated 5 September 1524. Tr. Walter Rauschenbusch, "The Zurich Anabaptists and Thomas Müntzer," *The American Journal of Theology* 11 (1905): 91-106. See also Eric W. Gritsch,

There were other groups which, like the Anabaptists, dissented from both Roman Catholicism and the mainstream of the Reformation associated with Luther, Zwingli, and Calvin. The Spanish physician Michael Servetus was the father of the "anti-trinitarians" who, on the basis of biblical evidence, denied the dogma of the Trinity. Since the denial of the Trinity also constituted a capital crime in the Holy Roman Empire, anti-trinitarians were as severely persecuted as were Anabaptists. Servetus was hunted through several countries until he was finally apprehended in Geneva where he was executed in 1553 with the blessing of Calvin.[7] The anti-trinitarian movement did survive, mainly by seeking refuge in the eastern corner of the Holy Roman Empire (Poland, Czechoslovakia, Hungary, and other regions in the East). Eventually, sixteenth-century anti-trinitarians merged with other unitarian movements.[8]

The Dutch Connection

Prevailing sixteenth-century notions of the imminent end of the world affected a variety of groups; Anabaptists were not excluded. Melchior Hofmann, a furrier who had become intrigued by the Bible's language about the end-time, joined the Anabaptists in 1530 and injected strong apocalyptic speculations into the movement by preaching and by writing numerous tracts. His followers soon became known as "Melchiorites" and could be found in Northern Germany and the Netherlands (then under the tutelage of Spain). These Melchiorites, or "comrades in the covenant" (*bontgenooten* in Dutch), distinguished themselves from other Anabaptist groups by remaining a secret party within Roman Catholicism; they were obedient to Hofmann's command to wait for the day when he, Hofmann, would be led to establish a new church which would be the

---

Reformer Without a Church. The Life and Thought of Thomas Müntzer, 1488-1525 (Philadelphia: Fortress, 1967), pp. 138-40.

[7]See Roland H. Bainton, *Hunted Heretic. The Life and Death of Michael Servetus, 1511-1553* (Boston: Beacon, 1960), chs. 9-11.

[8]See Earl M. Wilbur, *A History of Unitarianism*, 2 vols. (Cambridge: Harvard University Press, 1945-1952).

last Christian assembly on earth before the end-time. Hofmann had continued his speculations to the degree that he viewed himself as the new "prophet Elijah" who would lead the last group of Christians on earth. Emotionally exhausted and disappointed by the fact that the end had not yet come, he died a natural death in 1543.

The leader of the secret Dutch Anabaptist party was Jan Matthijs of Haarlem whom Hofmann had baptized. Matthijs in turn sent out twelve "apostles" to create an end-time community. Among those who joined the movement in the Netherlands was Obbe Philips who became an elder in the Friesland Anabaptist community. Jan Matthijs and Obbe Philips continued Hofmann's dream. They appointed several other "apostles" in Friesland; they believed themselves empowered to perform miracles and considered themselves immune to persecution. Obbe Philips ordained his own brother, Dirk, to the office of bishop in 1534. Both men produced a number of writings summarizing their various beliefs in the hope of attracting more followers.[9]

Some of their followers, led by Jan Matthijs, moved to the German city of Münster, near the Dutch border, where they persuaded the Lutheran pastor, Bernt Rothmann, to adopt Melchiorite ideas and programs. The radical wing of the Melchiorites soon won control of the city by emotional preaching and manipulation of the several thousand inhabitants. A political opportunist named Knipperdolling became the mayor of the city in February 1534, bringing to power with him several radicals who advocated the establishment of an "eternal kingdom" in the city. Within days, things had gotten out of hand. Twelve appointed "apostles" were led by a former innkeeper from Leiden, Beuckelsz, who introduced polygamy and ordered the execution of anyone who disobeyed him. "Prophet" Beuckelsz and "King" Jan married several wives, ordered all goods to be shared in common, burned all books except the Bibles, and established a reign of holy terror until the Catholic bishop of the

[9]For a summary of their lives and writings see *The Mennonite Encyclopedia*, 4 vols. (Hillsboro KS; Scottdale PA: Mennonite Publishing House, 1956), 2:65-66 (Dirke); 4:9-11 (Obbe). Hereafter cited *ME*.

region, Franz von Waldeck, besieged and conquered the city with the help of Protestant princes and their mercenaries in June 1535. The leaders of the "eternal kingdom" were executed, their corpses hung in iron cages from the tower of St. Lambert Church where they can still be seen today. Popular opinion, fueled by both Catholic and Protestant churchmen and politicians, quickly associated the "Münster affair" with the "Müntzer" who had incited riots among the peasants a decade earlier. Anabaptism had become synonymous with heresy, sedition, and rebellion.[10]

The Münster affair shocked Anabaptists everywhere. They wondered what had become of the initial commitment to non-resistance and pacifism. Among those who pondered the future was Menno Simons, a former Catholic priest whose brother had been martyred by Dutch authorities for having participated in revolutionary activities. Thus, on 30 January 1536, Menno Simons left his parish and joined the peaceful Melchiorites led by Obbe Philips. He was baptized by Philips and ordained an "elder" in the province of Groningen. For the next twenty-five years Menno Simons was to be the leader of an Anabaptist movement which vowed never again to violate its promise to remain pacifist. Simons traveled widely, first through Holland, then through northern Germany, and finally spent his last years as the revered leader of the "Mennonites" in Wuestenfelde, a small village between Hamburg and Leubeck. He was tireless in his oral and written reminders to keep communal discipline and to renounce force and violence. Like Luther, he presided over an international reform movement until his death in 1561.[11]

Dirk Philips continued Simons's work which was frequently threatened by dissensions and lack of communal discipline. His brother Obbe had intensified the use of the ban by the practice of

---

[10]On the "Münster Affair" see *ME* 3:777-83. Also John Horsch, "The Rise and Fall of the Anabaptists of Münster," *The Mennonite Quarterly Review* 9 (1935): 92-103; 129-43.

[11]On Menno Simons see Leonard Verduin, tr., *Menno Simons. Complete Writings*, ed. John C. Wenger (Scottdale PA: Herald Press, 1956).

"shunning," complete and active avoidance of those who had been banned because they had violated communal discipline. The practice of shunning continued in strict Mennonite groups which regarded seventeenth-century customs as unchanging norms of Christian living.[12] Obbe died in 1560, a disappointed and bitter man who had spent his final years in pious isolation. Dirk, beloved by the flock he shepherded from his residence in Danzig, died in 1568.

Anabaptist communities suffered severe persecution in the Netherlands during this period. Nonresistance and pacifism were as unpopular then as they are now. Anabaptists saw themselves as part of the long tradition of suffering which had begun with the persecutions of Christians by the Roman empire in the first century. Huterite and Mennonite chronicles depicted their own suffering as but one link in the chain of persecution ordered by both pagan and Christian Rome. The *Martyrs Mirror*, compiled in Holland in 1660, included hundreds of accounts of "the bloody theater" depicting the death of innocent Christians at the hands of those who claimed to be the orthodox defenders of Christian truth.[13] Dutch executioners, under Spanish order, killed men, women, and children in the name of Christ.

While Anabaptists were killed in the Netherlands, the Council of Trent (1545-1563) attempted to sort out the good from the bad in the Protestant Reformation. Catholic armies of the "Holy League" fought the Lutheran Smalcald League in 1546-1547; the resulting Peace of Augsburg in 1555 was a compromise which granted toleration to territories adhering to the 1530 Augsburg Confession. This toleration was not extended to Anabaptists. Calvin's model of a Puritan Protestantism, which he had created in Geneva upon his return to that city in 1541, was becoming more widespread. Lutherans, Calvinists, and Catholics were united only in their hatred of

---

[12]See John A. Hostetler, *Amish Society*, 3rd ed. (Baltimore: Johns Hopkins University Press, 1980).

[13]See Thieleman J. van Bracht, *The Bloody Theater or Martyrs Mirror of the Defenseless Christians*. . . . tr. Joseph F. Sohm (Scottdale PA: Herald Press, 1950).

Anabaptists whom they regarded as the seditious violators of mainline Christian traditions.

Nevertheless, Dutch Anabaptists were finally tolerated when, in their war of liberation against Spain, Dutch Calvinists succeeded in gaining independence for the Netherlands. The seven northern provinces of Spain became the Dutch Republic in 1579 through the Eternal Union of Utrecht. Calvinism was declared to be the state religion, but other Christian traditions, even Catholics and the Mennonite communities, were granted religious freedom.

Anglo-American Baptists

Anabaptists escaping persecution on the continent had crossed the English channel and sought safety in the British countryside as early as the 1530s. Catholic and Anglican bishops quickly linked them to the dissenting peasants, known as "Lollards," of the late fourteenth and fifteenth centuries. Many of these dissenters, among whom were both peasants and noblemen, had become followers of John Wyclif. Wyclif had called for the elimination of papal authority and had been labeled heretical in 1382, but did not suffer physical harm.

By the time Protestant teachings became popular in England during the reign of Edward VI (1547-1553), Anabaptism had become a sizable movement.[14] But neither the Catholic Mary Tudor, known as "bloody Mary" (1555-1558), nor the Anglican Elizabeth I (1558-1603) tolerated the "strangers" who had come from the continent; and James I (1603-1625), the first ruler over the united kingdoms of England and Scotland, strongly opposed all dissenters from the state religion of the "Anglican Church" (*ecclesia Anglicana*). As a consequence, those who rejected infant baptism and the episcopal structure as legitimate expressions of Christianity suffered severe persecution.

---

[14]See Irvin B. Horst, *The Radical Brethren. Anabaptism and the English Reformation to 1558*, Bibliotheca Humanistica & Reformatorica, 2 (Nieuwkoop: De Graaf, 1972), especially pp. 177-80.

Among those persecuted were "baptists" who, under the leadership of John Smyth, fled to the Netherlands in 1608. Smith considered infant baptism the mark of the false church and hoped to find a "true church" in the Netherlands. However, Amsterdam, where he and his group had gone, disappointed him. So in 1608 he rebaptized first himself and then his chief follower, Thomas Helwys, and thirty others. One year later, though, he changed his mind and applied for membership of his group into the Waterlander Mennonite community in Amsterdam. Thomas Helwys and a few other dissenting members of Smyth's group of Baptists decided to return to London and face persecution rather than join the Mennonites. They believed Smyth merely wanted to escape suffering. The Waterlander Mennonites did not admit the British Baptists until 1615, three years after Smyth's death.

The distinctions between Smyth's British Baptists and the Dutch Mennonites disappeared in the second generation when the children of the British immigrants had learned Dutch and were absorbed in the Mennonite tradition. The Baptists who had returned to London with Helwys survived. Like the Mennonites, they practised adult believer's baptism. Unlike the Mennonites, they thought political authorities were divinely instituted; they had no difficulty swearing oaths or serving in the army.

For many decades, the British Baptists, known as "general Baptists," and the Dutch Mennonites visited each other and exchanged their views in a number of publications. Various other Baptist groups also made contact with the Dutch Mennonites. One such group, under the leadership of Henry Jacob, developed Calvinist leanings and resided for a while in Zeeden, Holland; they were welcomed by the Mennonites. Once back in England, the Jacob group divided over the issue of how baptism should be administered and the "immersionist" faction sent a representative to a Mennonite community in Holland in order to be baptized by immersion. They were concerned about the apostolic succession of such a practice and the Dutch Mennonites were viewed as the guardians of its apostolicity.

British Baptists eagerly supported Oliver Cromwell's cause against the crown in the 1640s. Cromwell's death in 1658, however, brought a renewal of persecutions under the Stuart kings Charles II (1660-1685) and James II (1685-1688). The Toleration Act of 1689 finally ended their suffering and that of the other independent groups like Presbyterians and Congregationalists. They were never liked by the English crown, but could now flourish and communicate their distinct teachings and practices such as adult baptism by immersion, separation of church and state, and congregationalist polity. Following the Methodist revival in England, Baptists became involved in foreign mission and in 1792 sent their first missionary, William Carey, to India. They established the Sunday school movement, started Bible societies, and extended their mission to various parts of the world. John Bunyan, the author of *Pilgrim's Progress* (1628-1688), and Charles H. Spurgeon (1834-1892), the famed London preacher, attest to their popularity.

It was Roger Williams who in 1630 brought Baptist teachings to Massachussetts. He was a radical mind in his time, for he claimed what now seems to be commonplace, namely that no government has any control over matters of faith. American Puritans drove him out of Massachussetts. After having founded New Providence, Rhode Island, as the home for freedom of conscience in 1636, he returned to England and summarized his views in a treatise entitled "The Bloody Tenet of Persecution for the Cause of Conscience" in 1644. When he finally succeeded in creating a constitution which protected religious freedom in Rhode Island, the state became a haven for the Society of Friends, known as "Quakers." He and some of his followers had founded the first Baptist church in Providence in 1639, but he left the Baptist community to join the "seekers" who sought a Christian life devoid of all externals, including baptism, and who aimed at a mystical union with God.[15] He was the governor of Rhode Island from 1654 to 1657.

---

[15]There is a summary of the "seeker" movement in Rufus M. Jones, *Mysticism and Democracy in the English Commonwealth* (New York: Octagon Books, 1965), ch. 3.

Baptists were in America to stay. In 1644, Mark Lukar, another immigrant from Britain, founded another church at Newport, Rhode Island. From there, the Baptist movement spread to other colonies, notably to Massachussetts in 1649, Maine in 1682, Pennsylvania in 1684, and then into the South. Baptists were frequently jailed for teaching the separation of church and state. Only the states of Rhode Island and Pennsylvania really tolerated them. The revolution of 1776 granted them and all other religious groups the freedom they wanted to exercise, even though the Civil War again split Baptists into a Northern and a Southern division.[16]

Cruciformity Against Idolatry

Christians are always faced with the enduring problem of how to make the proper distinction between the First Commandment of the Decalogue ("I am your God, you shall have no other gods") and the temptation of the serpent "to be like God" (Gen. 3:5). There has been as much ecclesiastical original sinning as there has been sinning by narcissist individuals. The deification of culture has been a human trait ever since the beginning of recorded history. Eternal vigilance against the deification of self, of culture, and of nation has been the driving force of many reformations. Martin Luther opposed the ecclesiastical sin of selling salvation for a price, of receiving an "indulgence" for failures in this life as well as the next. But it did not take long for Lutheran territories to domesticate the gospel of the

[16]On Baptist history see Orland K. Armstrong, *The Baptists in America* (New York: Doubleday, 1979). On John Smyth see *ME* 4:554-55. The relationship between Baptists and Anabaptists is not yet well researched. My own preliminary research of sources in Holland indicates that there was considerable traffic of persons and ideas between British Baptists and Dutch Mennonites. See also Cornelius Krahn, *Dutch Anabaptism* (The Hague: Nijhoff, 1968). On continental Anabaptist and other "left wing" movements see Eric W. Gritsch and Roland H. Bainton, eds., *Bibliography of the Continental Reformation: Materials Available in English* (Hamden CT: Archon Books, 1972), "The Left Wing or Radical Reformation," pp. 124-58. Also Roland H. Bainton, "The Left Wing of the Reformation," *Journal of Religion* 22 (1941): 124-34; and George G. Williams, *The Radical Reformation* (Philadelphia: Westminster, 1962).

resurrected Jesus with Teutonic doctrine or pious confusions of faith and culture. Cultural Protestantism, be it Lutheran, Calvinist, Anglican, or whatever, had become a trait of Protestant history. The reformation for the sake of Christian priorities is a never-ending process. Sixteenth-century Anabaptists, Huterites, Mennonites, and seventeenth-century Baptists objected to what they perceived to be the idolatries of their time: the fusion of church and state; the baptism of infants; hierarchical episcopal and papal structures; violence—to name but the most significant vices of the established church. Yet Baptist reformers had difficulties with Baptist convictions. There were schisms and divisions over the proper exercise of discipline (be it banning or shunning) over questions of organization, and even over the mode of baptism (whether one should be immersed in, or sprinkled with, water). The idolatry of "being like God" lurks everywhere. No place and no time is safe from it, for the acceptance of the separation of human from divine power seems to be as difficult a matter as the notion that lamb and lion will sleep together.

Those who endured persecution in Zurich, Amsterdam, Augsburg, London, and all the other places listed in the accounts of the "bloody theater" of the sixteenth and seventeenth centuries, knew of the perennial Christian mandate to live in constant distinction, if not separation, from the "world"—the place and power which lures people away from the promise of salvation through the Christ crucified and resurrected. The history of the resistance to the world of narcissism, self-righteousness, and idolatry is a history of cruciformity; it is the story of a suffering people. Their "no" to idolatry meant a "yes" to cruciformity. Some of them were lonely reformers who fought a lonely battle against governments who wanted their soul. Others were well organized, indeed eager to fight might with might. The Swiss Brethren, the Huterites and Mennonites, the General and Particular Baptists, and their various branches were born in the conflict over Christian priorities. Their conflict was orthodox and necessary for it disclosed the enduring mandate of Christian discipleship: "He who does not take his cross and follow me is not worthy of me" (Matt. 10:38).

Chapter One

"WHERE ARE THE other ones?" Cecelia Geronymus asked.

"Gillis will not be here," Goris Cooman said. "I saw him yesterday in Hoorn. He said he will never see us again. He sends regrets, says to tell you that he is sorry. His terror of death is too much."

"Will he betray us?" Cecelia asked.

"He says that he will not. Maybe he is leaving because he cannot be sure. He has signed as a merchant seaman. Tomorrow he sails. To the East he thinks. Perhaps to China, though he is not certain. Anyway, he says he will never see us again. He says he is sorry."

"We have reason to be more sorry than he," Cecelia said, turning aside. "But then, even those who followed our Lord on earth would sometimes flee when times were trying. So might it be." She stood beside the window staring into the darkness, pretending to smooth the wrinkles from the broadcloth curtain as she spoke. "Gillis baptized more than three thousand of us. I among them. Also you and Pieter Boens." She sighed deeply and turned back to face Goris. "So we will beseech the Lord to latch his lips so perfectly that he will never incriminate his neighbors. There is the list you know. He has the list. Yes, my brother, we have reason to be sorry."

Goris spoke hurriedly. "Pieter will be here though. He is hiding the boat. We came together. He will canvass the docks to be sure we were not followed and be here shortly. You know he does not hear well now."

"Yes, I know." Her voice was calm as she moved back to the window. Goris continued as if he had not heard her, speaking in nervous gasps. "It was the molten lead. While he was their prisoner the margrave did it himself. When the bailiff could not make him talk, the margrave poured the sizzling potion into his ear, then cooled it at once with the water cup, sealing it forever shut."

"I know, Goris," Cecelia said again, her voice dropping to a whisper. "Yes, I know."

"Pieter said the margrave told him, 'You will hear no more of their seditious heresy from this ear.' Only the intervention of the bailiff saved the other ear from being seared as well." He was trying to speak more slowly, trying to be as calm as Cecelia appeared.

Pieter Boens entered the room while Goris spoke, embraced Cecelia without speaking and sat down.

"We will thank God for the bailiff's intervention," Cecelia said, looking directly at Peiter. "One ear is better than none."

"Thank God for whom you please," Pieter said. "But his intervention was not of mercy. He said that I could not hear their questions and could not confess if both my ears were sealed shut."

"Then we will thank God for their questions, won't we?" She said, touching Pieter playfully on the arm, glancing at Goris as she did.

Amsterdam was a city of harsh persecution in 1549. The same bitter wind had swept over most of the Low Countries and throughout Europe. The Calvinists and Lutherans had become the established church and were no more tolerant of those who disagreed with their doctrines than the Church of Rome had been with the Reformers not many years earlier. Lumping all dissidents together and calling them Anabaptists, the barbarities exercised on them knew few boundaries or limitations.

They were gathered in a large upstairs room in Cecelia's house. A short walk from the Amstel River, the house had belonged to her father, a lesser nobleman whose fortune was made from exporting grain. He had died of the plague almost two years earlier. Her mother died in childbirth. She lived alone on the inheritance from her father. For many years once each week a small group gathered in her house. They were generally people she did not know, had never seen before. They were recent converts and she taught them to read so that they could search and study the Scriptures. But this gathering was not a class. She had summoned Goris and Pieter herself. And for a special reason.

When she was a young girl she had been in a convent in East Friesia to learn the various arts and the Latin language. A servant in the convent gave her a Latin Testament. Partly from curiosity and partly from boredom with life in the convent she read it many times, often asking questions of the young woman who had given it to her. On her holiday she convinced her father to go with her to talk with a teacher in Amsterdam. He had told them of the Anabaptist faith. They were baptized the same day, not by the teacher but by Gillis, an itinerant elder who had recently arrived in the city.

Cecelia motioned with her head toward a loaf of plain bread which lay in the middle of a large oak table with benches on each side. Beside the bread were four pewter cups, each one more than half filled with red wine. With no signal and no announcement Cecelia began to sing, "I poor sheep on the green heath." Goris and Pieter joined in. When they finished singing Pieter moved to the table and broke the loaf into three pieces. Cecelia picked up one of the pieces and broke it again, placing it beside one of the cups. They stood together eating the bread and drinking the wine. There were no words, no ceremonies, and no blessing.

When they had finished Goris moved close to the table. "What of this?" he asked, pointing to the other cup and piece of bread.

"It is for Gillis," Cecelia replied. "Let it be."

"But Gillis is not here," Pieter said. "Goris said he will never see us again."

Cecelia took the remaining piece of bread and broke it in half, handing one piece to each man. "Then eat the bread," she said. "The wine will keep forever."

"Why not three pieces?" Goris asked. "Will you not share his bread?"

"Never mind the bread. Eat it and it will be gone. The wine will remain." She took the pewter cup and carefully poured the wine into a small decanter, filling it half full. When she had hid it in back of other bottles, cups, and earthenware utensils in a large oak cupboard, she turned to face them again. "It is there. Let it be. We have much to do."

Cecelia opened a door leading to a hallway and came back with a flat basket piled high with peat. With her bare hands she placed some of it on the tiny fire which had almost burned out, then emptied the rest into a tarnished brass scuttle. "It is from Velsen," she said, returning the basket to the hallway. "The bogs there seem to offer better peat now."

They returned to the table and sat down, Goris and Pieter on one side, Cecelia facing them in the direction of the fire. "I have word from Menno Simons," she said, almost whispering. "A letter." Pieter did not hear her and leaned across the table, turning his good ear. "Menno," she repeated a bit louder. "A letter. Blasius brought it yesterday from Emden." Neither man spoke. "He is going to Danzig. Wherever he goes those who give him shelter are persecuted, often killed. It is not in Friesland only. It is wherever he goes. He is crippled now, though he does not say how. He says that he cannot find in all the Low Countries a cabin or hut in which his poor wife and their little children can be put in safety for a year or two. But he does not whine. It is we who are his worry now. He warns us with his words. But also exhorts us to stand. He spoke of some long dead and some recently departed. John Walen and two of his fellow brethren suffered the most inhuman and tyrannous death, chained to stakes and a fire built near them but not on them, slowly parched until the marrow was seen to trickle down from their thighbones; thus being burned and roasted till death came to their relief. After their passage the garments on the upper part of their bodies were taken off piece by piece, the color of the cloth still being recognizable.

Hans Schlaeffer and Leonard Frick, Hans Feierer and eight others in Bavaria, drowned. He spoke of them and Hans Hut, found dead in his prison from smoldering straw in the tower, even then, dead as he was, carried in a chair on a wagon before the court where the corpse was sentenced to be burned. One must be present to be sentenced, you know. It must all be legal. George Bauman, George Gruenwald, Brother Alda, and George Steinmetz, all come to his mind, though they are dead for twenty years. And Lucas Lamberts, eighty-seven years old, his head placed upon a stake for all to see, his body on the wheel as food for the birds and wild beasts. Five years ago here in Amsterdam, an eighty-seven year old man. Killed in such fashion for his faith. Dirk and Samuel and Jacob, burned alive here three years ago. Pieter Jans, Tobias, Ellert, Barbara, Lucas and Truyken Boens, all burned alive at the stake on the same day one month passed. To warn us, Menno talked of all these. And more. But we who live are all his worry now."

At the names of the last six Pieter Boens began to weep. He had known them all, one by blood, had been imprisoned with them all, and had escaped the very day before their deaths. He told Cecelia how he had been freed. He had two friends living in Waterlandt, rough fellows he called them, who sitting drunk in a tavern planned a scheme for his release. They knew a man named Jan Jans who lived in the crescent opposite the prison. They took a basket containing a rope and well greased climbing block to his house in the morning and asked if they could leave it until it might suit them to come for it. In the dark of the evening they returned, threw a boat hook over the ledge, pulled themselves up the rope with the greased and silent block, broke open the window with a crooked iron and let their friend and the other prisoners they could find down the rope. Jan Jans agreed to the dangerous plan because his cousin, Ellert Jans, was also confined. But Ellert refused to escape, saying first that his wooden leg would make him easy to describe and he would soon be caught. In addition, he was so happy that he did not expect, even through a long life, to become any better; indeed, he feared that on the way through the long desert his courage might fail him and he would never get across the Jordan and reach the promised land.

"But now he has reached it," Pieter sobbed. Both Cecelia and Goris sought to comfort him but he turned away, saying that the age was too somber to indulge his own weakness.

"Someone must write it all down," Cecelia said. "And it is mine to do. I must tell of us. Not of doctrine. That is for Menno and others. But of the price. I know more than the rest. Not because I am greater, God knows the truth. But because I have heard more. For twenty years I have taught the new ones. Not what to believe but how to read. So that they may search the Scriptures and rightly divine the word of truth. And they have told me much. I must record if for their sakes. That is why I have called you here. We must write the story."

"How long before they come for us?" Goris asked. "Does Menno say?"

"He does not know," Cecelia answered. "Of time he knows no more than we. But he has read the signs. He knows what we know—that we are their lepers, their goats. They will come for us by their own clock, not by ours."

"What is it that you are asking us?" Goris asked. "Why have you called me here? I know of baking. Not of books. I hardly know the language. My mother was a Moor, brought from Spain by my soldier father as his bed slave, taken as his wife only when he came into the faith. And six years ago he died for that in Antwerp. And two days later she too, for no more offense than believing. My swarthy pelt is hers. My heart is of them both. Had I not been in Amsterdam I would have died with them. But tell me what more I can do than bake bread for the faithful."

"You can bring them here to me. You are of the city streets. Bring them to me. One by one or two by two. Each night I will see them. All of the faithful. Those who have been in prison, those who have seen the executions, those who have suffered persecution in whatever form, those who believe as we believe. By night I will see them and by day write it down until there is no more to tell or no more time, until they come for us."

"And what of me?" Pieter asked. Pieter was from Alsace, had studied for the priesthood in Paris, and later studied with Luther at Wittenburg. For a time he served as a Lutheran pastor, coming first to the Low Countries for that purpose. There he met Menno Simons. Since then he had worked as a proofreader for the leading printer in

Amsterdam. Because he spoke and wrote in four languages he helped with the placement of refugees in various countries. He was a small man and physically not very strong. Because he had so recently been in prison it would not be safe for him to be on the streets. Cecelia said that he would remain in her house, interpreting, editing, and sorting the materials they gathered.

She explained how they would proceed. First they must all agree on what was to be written. She had a list of questions which the three of them would discuss one by one. When they were of a common mind they would go to the next one.

"What do they call us?" she asked first, as if conducting a catechism class.

"Anabaptists," they both responded.

"Everyone?" she asked. "Does everyone call us Anabaptists?" No, not everyone, they agreed. The Calvinists and Lutherans did. And most of those in civil authority. But many in Amsterdam called them *Schwärmer*, fanatics. Some called them *Doopsgesinde*—baptism-minded. They preferred to be called Gospel-minded, for baptism was a minor concern. By now the Catholics called them hardly anything at all, seeing them more as reformers with bees in their bonnets—just due for the Lutherans and Calvinists who had so recently separated from Rome, to now have those of their own already disputing and breaking with them.

"Why do they call us Anabaptists?" Cecelia asked next.

"They say it is because we baptize one another when we are grown up, when we have already been baptized once before. When we were born," Pieter said. "But we do not really baptize a second time as they claim," he added.

Goris had moved to the fire and stood rubbing his hands. "Pouring a little water on a new-born baby's head is not really baptizing," he said. "He has made no commitment, stated no intention. And how could he be so filled with sin when he has done mischief to no one?"

"Except maybe his mother whom he kicked in the belly," Pieter laughed.

"If that be a sin it is one every woman wishes to have committed against her," Cecelia said. "Though surely no issue will come to me now."

"So we are wrongly named," Pieter said, serious now. "As well as unjustly accused. We are not rebaptizers as they claim. For what was done to us when we were three days old was not of our own choosing. We are simply baptizers. And should be so called."

"Then why do they call us that?" Cecelia asked. She had assumed the air and posture of both schoolmaster and scribe. Her quill moved quickly as they talked. She looked up only to ask a question or to speak to one they had asked.

Pieter and Goris had moved the small bench they shared closer to the fire, perpendicular to her, Pieter straddling it, his back to Goris, so that his good ear was in a line with them both. They spoke no louder than necessary to be heard.

"Is that why they hate us so?" Cecelia asked, not waiting for them to answer her last question.

"I think that is not why they hate us so," Goris answered. "Why would the Emperor Charles care what happens to our souls? And why would the despotic councils lift one finger to preserve our spirits? Our bodies, yes. But what advantage to them are our souls? If we go to hell for our heresy, what is it to them?"

"They care," Pieter said. "They cannot control our bodies unless they first control our souls. It is for their records. When they name us, number us, when they, as they call it, *baptize* us, they know who we are. We are theirs forever then. There is no king without subjects. And unless the king knows who they are, where they are, his vassals are soon gone. It is not the sign of Christ they put upon the little ones. It is the mark of Caesar."

"But why not simply enroll us? Declare us vassals by fiat? It would be so easy," Goris said.

"No more," Pieter said. "Now it is easier to do it in the name of Christ. Safer. For who will resist God Himself? Only the *Schwärmer*. And they will not stop until they have burned or drowned us all. And whether we be bakers, cutlers, tanners, chairmakers, ribbon weavers, barbers, or shoemakers, it makes no difference."

While Goris and Pieter talked to each other, Cecelia continued to write. When they stopped she looked up from her parchment and smiled. "Both of you are right and both of you are wrong," she said, moving toward the hallway for more peat for the fire. The chill of the night reached every niche of the room and a freezing rain rapped sternly on the shutters, making them groan and creak as the sheet of ice grew thicker upon them. "The river will be fixed solid by morning," she said, pealing the layers of peat onto the fire, poking it with her shoe toe until it flamed steadily. The two men waited for her to continue talking.

"It is true that they see our peculiar ways of baptizing each other as of no great gravity. But it is what they can use against us. For a thousand years it has been punishable by death to refuse to baptize the young. In the fourth century it was of convenience to the Empire after Constantine found the faith to be expedient. The other things they never bothered to make high crimes. They had not dreamed of them. It was for us to dream them, practice them, live them. Give them time and there will be laws for those as well. But for now they can only kill us for violating a decree which really bothers them little, except, as Pieter says, it helps them keep up with us. But it is for the other things they hate us most. Killing us for baptizing keeps them legal. It is true that they have no feeling for our souls."

Pieter nodded in agreement. Goris moved toward the door. "If you have all the answers already, why do you need us?"

"I have the same need of you that you have of me," she said, her voice even softer than before. "You are of me and I am of you. And there are few enough of us left. And you are on the list the same as I. Gillis baptized you too. And Pieter. They will come for you when they come for me. We will go together. But for now there is the story."

"Then you think they will get the list? What makes you think they will get the list?" Goris had moved back to the bench with Pieter.

"They will get the list. You may be sure they will get the list."

"What makes you so certain? You speak harsh words of our brother. Is Gillis not an honorable man?"

"You have spoken," she said, her voice still soft but somehow different. "Gillis is a man. There are different understandings of honor."

Pieter had turned his deaf ear to them and sat silently, shifting uncomfortably on the bench.

"Has he done you dishonor? Tell us! If we are of each other we deserve to know." He was trying to keep his voice down but couldn't.

"I am woman," she muttered. "We may have different understandings of honor. I will say no more."

Pieter stood up suddenly as if to warm himself. Goris, sitting on the very end of the bench, fell to the floor when Pieter got up, the bench striking him on the back as he fell. It was the first time they had laughed. Goris sat sprawled on the floor, making no effort to get up, giggling like a child. Pieter extended his hand and pulled him to his feet. The three of them stood in a circle, laughing more loudly than they had talked, jostling and hugging one another. "*Schwärmer*," Goris teased, poking Pieter in the ribs.

"*Schwärmer* yourself," Pieter said, stepping gently on his foot.

Cecelia stooped and lifted the baking kettle from the fire. She brought a small jar of tea from the cupboard and as she shook some of it into an earthen pitcher she said, "Too bad it doesn't grow in the bogs with the peat. It is almost gone."

"Perhaps Gillis will send us some from his journey," Pieter said.

Yes, perhaps so," Cecelia replied. "Meanwhile, help yourselves. We will not wait for Gillis."

As they blew into and sipped the black tea, Pieter grew more serious. "Tell us about the other things," he said. "The things they really hate us for. If it is not our baptizing."

Cecelia had stopped writing completely and was warming herself by the fire. Her body appeared frail but not her countenance. As she leaned forward, her loosely woven braids mingled with the flames before her and threw a flattering phantasm of her brow and bosom upon the far wall. Pieter looked at the shadow when he spoke, as if talking to another person.

"Well, let's make an agenda," she said, straightening upright, the image on the wall changing with her movements, then disappearing altogether as she moved away from the fire. "We will not serve on their juries, certainly that is disconcerting to them. But that is no big thing. There are many others, the Calvinists and Lutherans first of all, eager and more than willing to perform their patriotic chores. Of course, we will serve on the juries, too. But we will not swear by anything at all, we will not take oaths, so they will not let us serve. We will not go to war for any cause at all, will not serve in the armies of either the state or the Church. But I think they could tolerate that also. But there is the bigger issue." She moved to the table and made some quick notation upon the parchment, stood up, and paced the length of the room as she spoke.

"We do not agree that the state has the right to take the life of a person, no matter what the crime. Our reason is simple. Either a criminal has been saved or he hasn't. If he has been saved then it does not behoove us to take the life of a Christian brother or sister. If he has not been saved it does not behoove us to take any chance of salvation away by ending his life."

"Is this the big one then?" Goris asked, sitting nearer the center of the bench now.

"I think it is not the big one," she said. "I believe that they could even forgive us for our stance against the death penalty. After all, both the Lutherans and Calvinists, as well as the Catholics, recite each Sunday from the lectionary, 'O death, where is thy sting. O grave, where is thy victory.' But then they talk of death as a penalty. If death is a penalty then we are all doomed from the moment we leave our mother's womb. For we must all die. No, I think that is not why they hate us most."

She moved back to the table, sat down and motioned for silence. They watched her as she wrote. Her hand moved rapidly across the page, like she must finish in one instant... like she was writing things she had never thought before.

"It is enough for now," she said when she had finished. The rain had stopped and a steady wind pushed against the latticed shutters. "We will finish with the agenda tomorrow."

"What if they come for us tonight?" Goris asked.

"They will not come for us tonight," Cecelia said, a tone of certainty in her voice. "They always come when the weather is bright. They like pleasantness for their little outings. Anyway, it is late. And you must earn our bread. Pieter receives no salary for hiding out. And my leavings are dwindling fast. Pieter will tell you where he left the boat. When you return tomorrow you had best come on foot. Even if the river is not solid it is too risky."

Chapter Two

"ANY SIGN OF Gillis?" Cecelia asked when they had finished eating. It was a good supper. She had cooked a fish Goris brought and there was bread and jam. She poured them tea and they sat as they had before, Goris and Pieter on the bench, Cecelia at the table with her quill and paper. The sun had shone brightly all day and the fender of ice was gone from the shutters. A near full moon cast white beacons through the slats, aiding the two candles on the table as they struggled to light the room. "Any sign of Gillis?" she said again. "Did you hear any word of Gillis?"

"I saw him," Goris said. "They led him through the streets, his hands tied with a rope and his mouth tightly gagged so that he could not speak to those who followed or whom they passed on the way. The bailiff led him along like a calf, a chain fastened about his neck. They passed my shop. It was a sad sight, seeing him pulled along like that. A Lutheran preacher and some of his people mocked and poked him as they went, the bailiff making no effort to stop them. A woman in my shop said the armed horsemen had found him hiding in a barn in Haarlem. They were moving in the direction of a castle. I am certain that is where they took him."

The room was deathly quiet as he spoke, the faces of Cecelia and Pieter barren of any expression. The veins in Cecelia's neck stood out like the rambling route of a molehill, the muscles straining against her tightly gathered collar. Pieter breathed deeply and sighed as Goris finished.

"And now they have the list," Cecelia said at last. "Our time will not be long."

Goris made no effort to defend Gillis as he had the night before. "You may be right," he said. "At the market I heard that he had been released and that his ship sails tomorrow. I fear it is a bad sign."

"It is no sign at all," Cecelia said. "It is for certain. They have the list."

When persecution became severe and widespread against the Anabaptists, generally at the behest of the Lutherans and Calvinists, a plan was devised in Augsburg to make it harder for the temporal powers to convict them. Because it was sedition for one person to baptize another, except infants, the one who did the baptizing was in greater danger than the one baptized. Missioners were appointed who traveled from place to place, baptizing the converts who quite often did not know his name, nor him theirs. If they were caught and the bailiff asked, "Who baptized you?" they could reply honestly, "I do not know." And if he asked a local elder, "Who have you baptized?" he could say, "No one," and speak the truth. After the missioner had baptized all those in one place he would move on to another. For reasons of his own, Gillis had remained in Amsterdam for several years. The list of those baptized was kept by the itinerant missioner, so as not to endanger the local elder.

"But there is more news from the world, too," Goris said. "A woman, late in years, came to my door. She had with her a child, a bitsy girl. And with her a letter from the child's mother, Beliken Rogiers of Antwerp. Do you know her?"

Cecelia sat down, looking tired and faint. Pieter moved closer to where she sat, rubbing her hair as she sighed the way he had sighed, a lamentation.

"Yes, I knew poor Beliken," she said, starting to stand but sitting again, sinking into the chair. "She was my father's sister, only sister, much younger than he, almost my own age. She was in prison in Antwerp. Now you are telling me that she is dead. I know."

"Yes. I prayed for better news to bring you. But she was staked five weeks ago. Eight of them were taken while they were gathered to hear the word of God, taken before the burgomasters and judges and sentenced to death by fire when none of them could be turned from the steadfastness of their faith. I shudder to tell you of all this but the woman with the child insisted. She said you would rejoice in the great faith and strength of your kin. And that you could be proud of their deportment. Adriaen, your aunt's husband, preceded her by two months. She was spared for a time when a great dispute arose among the judges as to whether she should die when she was so far advanced in pregnancy. She did not plead for her life, only to be spared until her child should be delivered. The woman—she never gave her name—said she witnessed the execution of them both. When Adriaen came to the stake where he was to offer up his sacrifice, he kneeled down and offered up an earnest prayer to God, and then voluntarily prepared himself for death. But when the executioner was to strangle him, he could not find his twistingstick. The bailiff with his sword cut off a piece from the torch which they had to light the fire, that it might be used for a twistingstick. When he had been strangled, fallen sweetly asleep in the Lord, the fire was lighted to burn him. And just as this was taking place, the woman said there arose such a terrible storm that many people were frightened, and were of the opinion that God meant to show His displeasure upon the tyranny inflicted upon His elect. She said that Beliken had told her friends to bring the child to you, with this letter. She feared being followed to your house and came to my shop after dark. I did not tell her of our fear that we would soon be taken but said simply that I would bring her word to you. She asked that you read the letter, a letter written to her child the day before she was to die, the child also named Beliken."

Pieter had continued to stand beside Cecelia, occasionally touching her hair or patting her shoulder. She sat with her head back against the chair, her face drawn, but not crying.

"Do you want me to read the letter?" Goris asked.

"I will read the letter," she answered, extending her hand. "It is from my blood. It is for me to read."

Pieter moved to mend the fire, speaking dramatically to it as he did. "O riotous spirit of hearth and altar and executioner's stake. Who else, save man, can be such defender and devourer?" He sat on the bench as Cecelia unfolded the letter to its full length and began to read, his lips moving silently as he translated her words, sometimes to French, sometimes German, as if to absorb what he was hearing as many ways as possible.

A Testament Written To Beliken My Own Dearest Daughter, For A Perpetual Remembrance, Farewell, and Adieu From This Evil World, Written While I Was Confined For The Lord's Sake In Prison, At Antwerp A.D. 1549.

The true love of God and wisdom of the Father strengthen you in virtue, my dearest child; the Lord of heaven and earth, the God of Abraham, the God of Isaac, and the God of Jacob, the Lord in Israel, keep you in His virtue, and strengthen and confirm your understanding in His truth. My dear little child, I commend you to the Almighty, great and terrible God, who only is wise, that He will keep you, and let you grow up in His fear, or that He will take you home in your youth, this is my heart's request of the Lord: you who are yet so young, and whom I must leave here in this wicked, evil, perverse world.

My dear little lamb, I who am imprisoned and bound here for the Lord's sake, I who have but a few more hours upon this earth, can help you in no other way than to hold you up to the Lord. Your father and I were together such a short time, less than half a year, before we were apprehended because we sought salvation of our souls. They took him from me; and it was his great grief that I had to remain here in this prison. But now that I have abided the time, and borne you under my heart with great sorrow for nine months, and given birth to you in prison, in great pain, here I lie, soon to follow your dear father. And I, your dear mother, write you, my dearest child, something for a remembrance, that you will thereby remember your dear father and your dear mother.

Since I am now delivered up to death, and must leave you here alone, I must through these lines cause you to remember, that when you have attained your understanding, you endeavor to fear God, and see and examine why and for whose name we both died; and be not ashamed of us, dearest little one; it is the way which the prophets and the apostles went before us, and the narrow way which leads into eternal life, for there shall no other way be found by which to be saved.

My dear Beliken, I pray you, that wherever you live when you are grown up, and begin to have understanding, you conduct yourself well

and honestly, so that no one need have cause to complain of you. And always be faithful, taking good heed not to wrong any one. Learn to carry your hands always uprightly, and see that you like to work. And do not accustom your mouth to filthy talk, nor to ugly words that are not proper. And where you have your home, obey those whose bread you eat. You are but one month old, and they have kept me alive not to be with you but so that my flesh might heal from your leaving it (O that I could have kept you safe forever within my own flesh) before they offer that flesh up to be burned.

Please remember your dear father, and me, your dear mother, that we did not desert you but died that the world in which you live might be a better place. I leave you here among my friends; I hope that my niece, my brother's dear child, Cecelia Geronymus, may do the best with you as long as she lives. Be subject and obedient to her in every thing, so far as it is not contrary to God. I leave you the few guilders which my mother left to me. Read these words when you have understanding, and keep them as long as you live in remembrance of me and of your father. And I herewith bid you adieu, my dear Beliken, and leave you this letter along with a gold real, which I had with me in prison, these for a testament; that you may know of your family. I kiss you heartily, my dear lamb, with a perpetual kiss of peace. Follow me and your father, and be not ashamed to confess us before the world, for we were not ashamed to confess our faith before the world. Always keep this letter and this gold real for a perpetual testament, I herewith commend you to the Lord, and to the comforting Word of His Grace, and bid you adieu once more. I hope to wait for you; follow me, my dearest child.

Yet again once more, adieu, my dearest upon earth; adieu, and nothing more; adieu, follow me; adieu and farewell.

Written On The 10th Of October, A.D. 1549, at Antwerp. This
Is The Testament Which I Wrote In Prison For My Daughter
Beliken, Whom I Bore And Gave Birth To Here In My Bonds.
By Me Your Dearest Mother, Imprisoned For The Lord's Sake.

When Cecelia finished reading, she carefully folded the parchment and handed it to Goris who sat silently upon the hearth. Pieter sat upon the floor, his arms hugging the bench, his head buried upon them. His sobbing could be heard above the crackling of the fire and the branches of a giant elm tree which blew gently against the roof's edge with predictable timing. The oscillating sounds of a wood pinioned clock made their way up the stairs from the living quarters and into the room. Those were the only sounds. Cecelia sat staring into the fire, making no motion except the heaving of her heavy breast. She had not whimpered during the entire reading of the

letter, reading slowly and almost matter-of-factly. Her voice never faltered, never wavered. And it did not now as she crossed the room and placed her hand on Pieter's head.

"It is appropriate that you cry, Pieter," she said. "And perhaps I, too, will cry. But it is in the fashion of which our Lord spoke: 'Weep not for me you daughters of Jerusalem, but weep for yourselves, and for your children. For, behold, the days are coming, in which they shall say, "Blessed are the wombs that never bear, and the paps which never gave suck."' My womb is so blessed. Or so cursed. I suppose the line is sometimes thin. But though we wait and howl, go stripped and naked, make wailings like the dragons, and mourning as the owls, it will not advance our present task. It would be folly and deceive no one to bring the child here now. We must write the story. For now they have the list."

She returned to the table and made notes of the letter and of what Goris had told them of Gillis. She pretended to write even after she had finished, giving Pieter and Goris time to put their thoughts in order. To divert his mind she asked Pieter to bring up more water for the kettle. When that was done she noted a mouse which had been scampering about the room, looking for the spot where he had entered. Goris moved to smash him with the stoker from the hearth but Cecelia asked him to chase him through the hallway door. "Thanatos is too much with us already," she muttered, continuing to write. "Let him live." Goris shrugged and sat down.

"Very well," she said at last, placing her quill in the well. "We were talking of what it is about us they hate the most. We will not baptize our young because it is nothing more than the state's manner of enrolling them. We believe the state and the fellowship of the faithful should never be one. We will not kill for them and will not swear in their courts so we cannot be their judges. If these things are not the true reason for their persecution, then what is? What is our most heinous crime in their estimate of us?"

Goris and Pieter had returned to the bench before her, sitting like schoolboys. "I believe you have asked a question which you will now proceed to answer," Goris said. "So tell us."

"I can but tell you what I believe," she said.

"Then tell us that."

"There is one thing, a thing which we do not really do, save when because of their persecution they force us to it. But it is that which they fear the most. It is that which strikes at the heart of the sovereign and feudal systems, and they will not abide us because of their fear of it."

Pieter raised his hand to be recognized. "You need no permission to speak, dear Pieter."

"It is community of goods," he said, his smile widening to a grin as Cecelia nodded her head in approval. "They call us communists," he said, "der Kommunist, Communiste, Communist!" shouting now, saying the word in three languages.*

"I have known it for a long time," he continued. "I was in Tirol, and also in Moravia when Jakob Hutter was leader there. And it is true that the brotherhood there was communistic, but it was necessary for their survival. Everywhere they saw the blood of the martyrs and the burning stakes, prisons filled with captives, children forsaken and starving at home, they themselves driven into the fields like herds of sheep, there to lay down on the wide heath under the open sky with many wretched widows and children, sick and infants. They meant harm to no one. What was their choice but to combine their goods. Good news for the poor must surely mean, at the least, food for their bellies. So the temporal gift, a sweet sacrifice, a little food for the faithful, had to be. Threatened with hangmen and bailiffs, the Sodomite sea raging so madly, what else could they do? But precisely because it proved to be their greatest defense they were hated and feared the more for it, by Sovereign Ferdinand and feudal lords. And the pious Jonah had to be cast into the sea. And was. Yet the brotherhood survives."

He had stood when Cecelia nodded, and as he spoke he strode the length and breadth of the room, his hands reaching to the ceiling, his arms flailing and thrashing as he preached, his voice pitched to a near scream.

---

*The use of the word "communism" to describe a political system did not occur until much later.

Cecelia's face was a blossom of pride, like a teacher hearing the recitation of a favorite pupil. Her hand and quill moved across the page like sails driven by the wind. When Goris spoke she did not stop, letting the two of them exchange their thoughts, writing it all down.

"But that is not our practice here," he said. "We do not urge one another to sell our property. We have no common treasury. I know that we have been accused of everything from trying to destroy the city of Amsterdam when forty rebels aimed a double loaded artillery at the guildhall where all the magistrates were gathered, to trying to take over the entire army of Charles II. All that despite the fact that one of the crimes they say we commit is refusing to bear arms, and I know that those who write their stories will record that we did those things. All the more reason why Cecelia must finish her story. But what profit to them to say that we are communist when we are not? To us it is love. For them it is sedition. Even here. In this house. Do you forget that it is your food that we eat, Cecelia's shelter and fuel which warms us? And I, because of what they have done, because of circumstance, I contribute nothing. To them that is der Kommunist."

"But you contribute much," Goris said. "And in the days to come, more. As for the food I bring, my shop is as much yours as mine. And Cecelia's shelter is the same. Of that I am certain. We are communitarians, but we are not der Kommunist."

"Yes," Pieter replied. "Yes. So it is. And that is what they fear most. It is community which they fear will be their undoing. Love is always without condition, while the sovereign state is never without its bridle to guide us where it wishes. And control the gait."

"But it is their churches which accuse and oppose us most. More than the temporal powers," Goris answered.

"That is because the two of them are one," Pieter said. "That is what our sister is writing. As long as the two of them are one there can never be community. There will not be Church. There will only be State."

Cecelia stopped writing abruptly and stood up. "The foundation is laid," she said. "We have done the proem. Now we must start the text. It will be written. Tomorrow is the sabbath. Where do we gather?"

"At Harlaan's tannery," Goris said.

"Pieter must remain here. You will make the arrangements for all who attend the gathering to come here for the interviews."

When Goris had gone Cecelia and Pieter sat at the table facing each other. For a long time neither spoke. Then they talked a while of trivial things . . . Should they bring more peat from the cellar. . . . How had the mouse got into the hallway. . . . How long until all the canals and rivers would be frozen solid. . . . How old the tree was which continued to blow against the roof. Pieter studied her handsome face, the long braids of her flaxen hair, falling primly about her rounded shoulders like fine linen, the circled lines upon her high cheeks, looking like annual rings of a maple tree cut too soon. Who could contrive to do her evil?

"Do you think I do wrong?" she asked breaking a long silence. "Has my zeal become my sin? The devils have such guile. Tell me if I err. Will you chasten me if I misgo, Pieter? I think I could not bear rebuke from you. But, God knows I do not stand above your admonition. It is a plea I make of you, a solemn entreaty. You must tell me."

"With my one good ear I hear you," he said, turning partly away. "But my heart does not know what you ask."

"The story," she said, impatiently, almost angrily. "My decision. I made it as if there was no choice to make. I chose the story over my own blood, over poor little Belikan, my own flesh. I did it so quickly. But it is my passion, Pieter." She walked to the window and peered between the slats, pushing the curtain aside as she did, without turning around she said as if to herself, for she knew Pieter could not hear, "I hope it is my call as well." Then, turning to face him she said, "I know it is my obsession, Pieter. But now you must tell me if it is also my curse." She sat again upon the bench.

Pieter moved around the table and placed both his hands on her shoulders. She did not move. "Truth is the highest thing that men may keep, wrote a lettered Briton. And another one, close kin to us, said that he believes that in the end the truth will conquer. That is what you wish to do?"

"That is what I wish to do," she whispered close to his ear.

Chapter Three

CECELIA SAT STUDYING the man and woman sitting directly across from her at the table. Goris had brought them and left immediately. Pieter made them tea and banked the fire, then sat close enough to hear well so that he might translate some of Cecelia's words into their native German. Cecelia had seen them both at their gatherings and knew them by name. She made notations on the paper spread upon the table. "Jerome Dircks . . . came here from Augsburg . . . fifty-one . . . rather tall . . . light brown cropped hair . . . blond mustache . . . dressed in black ridingcoat, broad gray hat, and gray pants . . . weaver of wool."

She had greeted them properly when they came and as she made them welcome explained what she, Goris, and Pieter were about. The man agreed but the woman cautioned her of the danger, that it could get her in bad trouble with the burgomasters. She suggested that it might be a better plan for Cecelia to go to the homes and shops of those she would talk with rather than have a steady trek to her own house. Cecelia assured her that they would take the usual precautions, that Goris knew the city well and would not use the same route each night. She also explained about the list, that they might not have much time.

Even before Cecelia finished her notes of their physical appearance Jerome Dircks began to speak. "I must tell you that I was baptized in Münster."

"Then you do not know Gillis?" Cecelia asked.

"I know him but I was not baptized by him. I was baptized by Willem de Cuyper who came to Münster from Haarlem."

"At least that much is good," Cecelia said. "At least you are not on the list and are a bit safer than most of us. I am certain that the bailiff has the list now."

"But I did not take part in the rebellion in Münster," he added hastily, ignoring what she said about the list. "I was a young man then but already a weaver. I left as soon as the fighting started."

"Do not apologize for anything," Cecelia told him. "I am not interested in myths. I do not wish to construct a network of fabrications. No offense, but I am not a weaver. I know of what happened in Münster. It is in no way an embarrassment to me. Is it to you?"

"Not an embarrassment," he said. "But I did not then consider them, as they call us, Anabaptists, and I do not now."

Cecelia glanced up from her paper to ask, "Why?"

"Because they resisted with violence. In their zeal they resorted to the sword. And that is not in our teachings." He looked quickly at his wife sitting silently beside him, put his hand on hers and continued. "And though I had taken no wife at the time, I had more than a little trouble with their holding of wives in common."

"Of property? Of goods?" Cecelia asked. "Did you agree with that?" She spoke rapidly and he did not understand. Pieter first repeated the Holland Dutch words, then pronounced them in German.

"I did not practice it in the same fashion as they. I was not a prosperous man but such as I had I shared freely with the brotherhood. But no, I had no trouble with that."

Cecelia continued to write and now she talked at the same time. "Tell me about Münster. About the rebellion. My own mind is the same as yours. I weary of the Catholics and the reformers continuing to whip us over the head with Münster, to abuse us with the folly of

Münster as their excuse. I do not think they were of us either. I too was young at the time but my father told me much about it. Put it in your own words. What did you see? Perhaps some of it will fit the story, even though they were not of us."

Jerome did not move as he talked. Pieter, seeing that Cecelia was having no difficulty with his speaking, left the room to check on a noise he heard on the outside. Finding a pig rooting for grubs in the yard, he chased him off and came back.

"Well, I don't remember all the details," Jerome said. "But really what was going on was some Lutherans got halfway converted by some Anabaptists. I mean, they took the part about not baptizing infants but that's about as far as they got. And times were hard. A lot of persecution of the true believers and sometimes these halfway Lutherans too. Anyway, this man Rothmann was a powerful preacher and recruited hundreds of ignorant and simple people who were very, very poor. He told them that he had word from God to set up a new Jerusalem in Münster and they formed themselves into a sizeable army. But when they set up fortifications and moved to take the temporal power from the bishop of Rome and the civil authorities, the poor peasants were slaughtered and their leaders either killed or taken prisoner for an even worse and more shameful experience. When it came to such a quick and certain end the Lutherans, the real Lutherans, placed the blame for it on the Anabaptists. If it had been successful, if the city had actually been taken over by this wicked and unscriptural revolt they would gladly have taken the credit but the persecution of the Anabaptists would have gone on just the same. All that is what I think, not what I know. But it is plain that they were not of us."

Cecelia made few notes while he was talking of Münster. It was as if what she heard was old and familiar and of no interest to her. Her inquiring glance at Pieter told him she had heard the noise outside. He shrugged and said, "A pig."

"Well, I suppose he is not one of their spies. Too bad we can't chase the demons of Amsterdam into him the way Jesus did among the Gaderenes."

"I have never condemned the Münsterites as some have," the

man continued. "They were, of course, wrong and not of us, to take up the sword. But there was considerable justification for what they did. It is hard to speak enough of the torment they had known. And when the leaders railed against the lords it was easy enough to be persuaded."

Cecelia corrected him as he spoke. "There can never be justification for resorting to the sword, my brother. But enough of Münster. Tell me of Augsburg."

"I had a friend there, a faithful brother named Gerrit Hasepoot, a tailor by trade and a good one too. I left Münster to go to him, thinking that I could supply the wool for his shop. But when I arrived I discovered that because of severe persecution he had fled the city. But within a brief time he returned in secret, since his wife and children were still living there. He was seen by the bailiff's guard who reported it to his master. The bailiff, a very bloodthirsty man, immediately went after and captured him. When he was severely examined by the lords of this world and the priests of this world as well, he freely confessed his faith and was not ashamed. He was sentenced to death by them, that is, to be burnt at the stake, a sentence he received bravely. This having taken place, his wife came to him, into the city hall, to speak with him once more, to take leave, and bid her dear husband farewell. She had in her arm an infant which she could scarcely hold because of her great grief. When wine was poured out to him, as is customary to do to those sentenced to death. . . ."

"Wait a minute," Cecelia said. Turning to Pieter she asked, "What is that Proverb about wine for the dying? It will fit here. Will you find it for me?" A huge Lutheran Bible rested upon the cupboard. Pieter walked over, opened it up, and began to search while Cecelia continued to write what the man had said, asking him twice to repeat something he had told her.

When she stopped writing Pieter read the verse: "Give strong drink unto him that is ready to perish, and wine unto those that be of heavy heart."

"Yes that's the one. They can be so tender. Give you wine when they pronounce the sentence. Or wait for the lacerations of childbirth to heal before they put you to death."

The man continued to talk when he saw that she was ready. "My friend said to his wife: 'I have no desire for this wine; but I hope to drink the new wine which will be given to me above in the kingdom of my Father.' Thus the two separated with great grief and bade each other adieu in this world. The woman could hardly stand on her feet any longer, but seemed to fall into a swoon through grief. When he was led to death, having been brought from the wagon upon the scaffold, he lifted up his voice, and sang the hymn:

Father in heaven, I call:
Oh, strengthen now my faith.

"I had gone to the execution because his wife asked me to walk alongside him, that she could not bear to see him die, and thought it best that she remain with the children. Several times he called out to me and others of the faithful he recognized as the wagon brought him to the scaffold: 'Brethren, sisters, all, good-bye! We now must separate.'

"When they took him from the wagon and placed him at the stake, he fell upon his knees, and fervently prayed to God. One who assisted the executioner came forward with gunpowder, pouring and sprinkling it heavily upon his beard and dusting it in his hair. Seeing me nearby in the crowd he called out, 'They have salted me good, my friend,' not addressing me as brother and not calling my name aloud. When they began to secure him to the stake he kicked his slippers from his feet, saying: 'It is a pity to burn them for they can be of service still to some poor person.' The rope with which he was to be strangled became a little loose, having not been twisted well by the executioner's aid whose job it was to put it in place. The executioner, speaking harshly to his aid and showing great impatience, began twisting the rope a second time, Gerrit singing the end of the hymn as he did:

Till we meet beyond the sky,
With Christ our only Head:
For this yourselves prepare,
And I'll await you there.

"With those words on his lips he fell asleep in the Lord, having fought the good fight, finished his course, and kept the faith."

All the time he spoke he kept his fingers laced tightly in the hand of the woman beside him. She sat straight and rigid, showing no sign of emotion as he spoke, watching the quill in Cecelia's hand as it danced along the lines, seeming otherwise oblivious to what was going on about her. The tea which Pieter had placed before them had grown cold as neither had touched it. He offered to warm it in the kettle but they drank it as it was, sharing together all that was in one cup, then drinking from the other. Pieter sat looking over Cecelia's shoulder, occasionally putting German words into Holland Dutch, leaning close to hear her questions. The woman and man across the table spoke to each other in whispers as Cecelia continued to write.

She took a fresh leaf, studied the woman's countenance again and jotted notes. Barbel Dircks . . . medium build . . . lathy, eggshell skin . . . full blond hair in bun . . . appears older than Jerome.

"Now. Tell me about yourself," Cecelia said to the woman somewhat condescendingly. "Just tell me whatever you want to tell me."

"I was the wife of Gerrit Hasepoot," the woman said, without emotion. "Jerome and I were married a year after they killed Gerrit."

Cecelia placed her pen in the well and asked her no more questions. For a long time they talked of pleasant things, ate bread and cheese, took turns singing songs of their native countries and making up limericks. Pieter was awarded the imaginary prize with his offering:

There once was a woman from Haarlem
Whose faith brought on quite an Alarum.
The baliff came by,
Upon her to spy,
And was met at the door by ole Charon.

Their laughter warmed and filled the room. Margraves and executioners were for the moment beyond their concern.

"Life was so good," Cecelia said as she bid each of them good-night.

"Life *is* so good," Pieter said when they were all gone.

Chapter Four

CECELIA HAD ADOPTED her project as if it were a foundling baby, something which was not of her planning, not a part of her own self, yet now hers completely. And like an unexpectant foster parent frantically thrashing about for a borrowed bottle, a put-away bunting, or long neglected crib before settling into a routine of her own, now that the objective had been established, the project was never out of her sight and care. She arose from her sleep with the last line of the night flowing steadily into the first words of the morning. She hurried to begin each day. A room so nearly empty would be a gray place as a writer's studio for most but for her it was enough. She leaned upon Pieter for quick translations, for needed Scriptures, dates of events and places hazy in her own mind, and upon Goris to keep the flow of witnesses to her door. With these two to assist her and with this fire in her bosom, she stitched the worded quilt piece by piece, as if convinced that it would be the one to thaw the icy bed of falsehood and tyranny upon which they lay.

Only one man had been brought on this night. She had completed the interviews with those in their own little fellowship and now Goris was reaching out for others—travelers coming through

Amsterdam from other towns and countries, recently arrived fugitives seeking asylum in the Low Countries, or someone who happened by his shop. The one before her now was an exile from Zurich, driven out, he said, when the Zwinglians said he must stop preaching.

"How were you baptized?" Cecelia began.

The man told his story. "I do not know his name. The man who baptized me. I was traveling from Zollikon and rode along with a kind man who said he was a shoemaker from St. Gallen. He had been a follower of Zwingli but had disputed with him about his pagan superstitions pertaining to baptism, all the blowing, driving out of the devil, crossing, moistening with spit, and anointing with oil. He told me there is nothing in the Scripture which mentions all those accessories. I must say that I had wondered about the same things myself. As we rode, stopping once at night for rest, he taught me of the Anabaptist faith. I was filled with a new and strange warmth. We stopped at the village well of Hirslanden where two other men were waiting. At first I feared that they had come to apprehend him but soon saw that they were friends. A veil seemed to lift from my eyes as they talked. Finally I said to my traveling companion whose name I did not know and do not now know, 'Very well then, my friend, you have shown me the truth. Now I am asking you for the sign.' 'Are you asking to be baptized?' he said. 'Yes,' I replied. 'I am asking for the sign.' And then he baptized me."

"How did he do it?" Cecelia asked. "Tell me every word and every motion. Leave out nothing. Do not assume that I know anything at all. Exactly what did he do?"

"Here is what I remember. And I think it is all that happened that day at the well. He asked if I was heartily sorry for all my sins and I replied that I was.

" 'Do you desire the baptism?' he asked me. 'Yes,' I answered. 'Who will forbid me, that I should baptize him?' 'No one,' the two others replied together, my friend saying the words along with them. 'Humble yourself before God and His Church and kneel down,' he instructed me."

The man knelt down between the tables as he talked. "He took a metal dipper, not the large one which was at the well but one he had tied upon his saddle, a small one such as you might have in your kitchen. He filled the dipper with water from the well and poured it over my head as I knelt, saying, 'I baptize you in the name of God the Father, God the Son, and God the Holy Spirit.' And that is all that he said."

Cecelia continued to write as the man stood up and returned to the table. Pieter sat awed beside her, like one witnessing the finale of an exciting drama.

"There was no crossing, oil, blowing, no saliva, no driving out the devil?" she asked, continuing to write.

"There was none of that," the man said.

Goris had returned to the house with three other people, two women and a man. They stood on the landing brushing the snow from each other's backs. Pieter did not move to greet them and hang their coats as he generally did. His eyes had not moved from the spot where the man had knelt. Goris brought them inside and took their coats to the hallway himself, returning with peat for the fire, and a little wood. Cecelia did not look up from her tablet, did not even nod as the four of them moved about the room, totally absorbed in what she wrote. When she finished she explained the project to the strangers without greeting them. And without rising.

"Have any of you been in prison?" she asked.

"Yes," all three responded.

"Who among you has been tortured?" she asked. "I will speak first with you."

The man moved forward and took his place at the table facing her. "Before we begin there is something I must tell you," he said. When he talked there was a shrillness in his voice, a soft whistling coming from his throat with the words, like wind blowing over a reed. He was a short man, very thin, with scant red hair and thread-like beard. His eyes sat far back in his head but they were warm and kind and looked like agate as he spoke.

"What is your name?" Cecelia asked, ignoring what he had said to her.

"My name is Jacob Cool. But there is something I must say to you before we begin."

Cecelia wrote the name and nothing more. It was as if there was some mechanism in her mind which silenced and redirected any words not having to do with her questions. She did not appear agitated, simply writing the name down, then moving on to the next question.

"Where are you from, my brother? I can tell that you are from the Low Countries."

The man smiled and reached across the table, placing one hand upon hers, gently lifting the feather quill through her fingers with the other one. "I understand your dedication and devotion," he said patiently, holding the pen away from her reach. "And I come to you in all goodwill. But there are things more important than your project."

"What?" she snapped, impatient and irritated at this delay.

"That of which you write is more important than whether or not you write it. What was, is, and will be. You seek to conquer them with your words of truth. And well you might. But conquering, winning is a dangerous thing. For the victors seem always to accept the gods of the vanquished. Can we not see it in what has happened to us? The reformers have won over the Papists throughout Europe. Everywhere the people saw and believed and followed because of the oppression and corruption of the Roman Church. But before their castles were even aired out, the reformers had inhabited them and now use no different methods to oppress and persecute us." He spoke calmly and with no anger, but there was a sternness about him as he spoke.

"Is that what you wished to tell me," she asked, not quite so testy now.

"No," he said. "What I want to tell you before I begin is that within their understanding of truth they can justify the persecution, even the torturing of us. It is not that they are liars and rogues that they do these things. Your honor, your integrity, your passion for truth are all admirable things. But they may also become idols. It is God who must be honored, not our honor which must be honored. This, I fear, is where Luther has missed the way. And Calvin and

Zwingli as well. They all taught that we are saved by faith. But suppose I cannot have faith any more than I can do good works. Am I then damned? Eternally damned? I say you nay."

Goris had finished his chores and stood attentively before the fire. Pieter looked at the man with astonishment. "How then are we saved?" he asked, trying to mask the irritability he was feeling.

"It is by faith. As Luther says," Jacob replied, still calm. "But it is not my faith. It is the faith, the faithfulness, of God."

"By that logic then how do we differ from the Roman Church?" Pieter said, standing up now, his voice rising with him. "Why could we not simply have said, 'We are saved by good works but it is not *my* good work but the good work of God which redeems us.' Then we could all be good Catholics again."

"Perhaps we could," Jacob sighed. "Yes, perhaps the line is that thin. But what I want to say to Cecelia before we begin in earnest is that when they torture us they do not say it is because they hate us. They say it is because they love us, even as we say we love them."

Cecelia sat quietly now, tapping in rapid cadence with her fingers upon the table, irritated anew at his preachments. Pieter had walked to the other side of the table and stood behind the man.

"How can they say they love us and still torture us the way they do? I have been in their prison. As you say you have. Perhaps your experience was more pleasant than mine. But I saw no mark of love in it."

"Yes, perhaps mine was more pleasant than yours," the man said. "I will tell you of it in a moment and then you may judge for yourself. I simply wished to say to our sister that the reason they use to justify our torture is that they are trying to drive the demons out of us, that we are possessed, that demons inhabit our bodies, and if they can make existence within our bodies intolerable, the demons will depart and we will be restored to our senses."

"Demons! Demons! What demons? Do you think we are possessed? What an excellent defense for Judas!" Pieter said. "He was willing to hand the Lord over to the soldiers because they thought they were doing good, thought they were honorable men." He was shouting down at the man now. "What do you say to that?"

Jacob had not turned his head and continued to speak with the same composure as before. "I say that there seems now to be schism brewing amongst us. If we permit that to happen... well, how are we different from them? It makes my point well. Just remember that even the devils have their honor. And their zeal. Let the story be told. I have no doubt that Cecelia is writing it well. But let us remember that the telling of the story is not the story." He continued to look at Cecelia, as if he were speaking only and directly to her, and repeated the last words. "The telling of the story is not the story."

Cecelia sat for a long time, saying nothing. Her gaze was one of consternation, tempered by a mild and grudging awareness that what she had just heard was worthy of consideration. She drew back slightly but only for a moment, then leaned closer to him, studying his pale gray eyes.

One of the women had unwrapped a large and very stale croissant from her handkerchief and was offering to share it with the others. Cecelia took a small bite and passed it on, still not taking her eyes off the man before her. Pieter sought to compose himself by fixing tea for everyone. As he moved about the room he asked the man to forgive him for his impatience.

"It is just that we probably have so little time. When the crocuses come, they will come too. If not before. They have the list."

"I understand," the man said. "I am ready to begin."

"Where are you from?" Cecelia asked again. It was as if there had been no interruption in her questioning at all.

"I am from here. I am from Amsterdam. I studied in Marburg. To be a doctor. I wanted to be a physician as my father is. But I was arrested before my studies were complete. I can stay in Amsterdam because I live in my father's house and leave only at night. He is not one of us but he will not betray us."

He seemed old to have a living father. "How old are you?" she asked, then was sorry when he answered, "Twenty-six." She had thought he was fifty. Jacob smiled behind his sparse beard, knowing what she was thinking.

He began his story in the third person. "He had been to Antwerp and was returning home. Nearly a league from the castle, he met the judge who saluted him and rode past. He thanked the judge. . . ."

"Are you speaking of yourself or of another?" Cecelia interrupted.

"I am telling of what happened to me," he replied.

"Then please tell it that way. It makes the writing easier."

"I thanked the judge, satisfied that he did not know me. But then the actuary rode up to me, asked me where I was going and what I had been doing. I replied that I had been with my brethren. He asked if the Anabaptists were my brethren. I told him they were. The actuary then seized me and the judge rode back to us, dismounted, and taking my own girdle from my body, bound me with it and made me walk like a dog alongside his horse, through mud and mire, for a whole league, until we arrived at the castle. I was so fatigued from the walking and from being bound so hard, that I could stand no longer and fell down in the field. Even the lord of the castle reproved the judge for having bound me so hard. They examined me on the spot, taking all my possessions from me, and put me in prison. The next day the lord of the castle examined me himself, asking questions concerning my faith, baptism, and what I thought of the sacraments. The lord did not harm me but pressed me hard to recant. When I told him that one did not recant the truth and did not confess to error when no error existed, they took me back into prison.

"Eight days later I was brought out again and examined by the lord and six others. When I did not answer the questions to their satisfaction, I was again remanded to prison. After another eight days I was arraigned before the whole council. The judge called our faith a delusion, brought to us by demons. He called our church a sect. I told him that it was neither a sect nor a delusion but the church of God. The judge said that it was the devil's church and not God's. I made no answer when he said such things, dealing only with the questions they addressed to me. The judge then said that since I knew who had come to Amsterdam from the seigniory of Innsbruck, I must tell them the names of all who had come, where they were, and who had fed and harbored them."

"Did you know those things?" Cecelia asked, pausing in her dictation.

"Yes," the man said. "I knew all those things." When he had spoken in the third person it was with excited gestures and intonations, but when the pronoun changed he had changed with it, speaking now in a halting monotone, the whistling from his throat serving as punctuation breaks.

"I knew but I explained that I did not wish to tell them, could not accuse or betray any one. I asked the judge and the whole council if they would consider a man good if he became the instrument leading to their torture. They agreed that they would not but the judge became enraged, said that I was accusing them of requiring treachery of me. When I would not answer they took me to the rack. I removed my clothing myself and patiently submitted to the torturing ropes which they attached to my shoulders, ankles, knees, and thighs. They placed a sizeable rock upon my groin, so that when the wheel was turned to stretch me the rock dug into my flesh. The pain cannot be described. It was so great that the eyes of the bystanders were filled with tears. When I would not answer their questions the bailiff said that perhaps water would flush out the demons within me. A pipe was inserted into my mouth with a flange and funnel attached which left no place for the jars of water they emptied into it to go except into my own body. When my stomach was overflowing it began to run into my lungs so that I fell into great convulsions and thought that I would surely die. Even as I retched and strained the judge railed at me. 'You swear to each other that you will not betray one another.' I could not tell him that we do not swear at all. 'You are a rogue! I have detected you in a lie. Why will you suffer yourself to be tortured?' In my fainting his voice seemed far off in the distance. 'You said that you were no teacher, but we find that you are. You even seek to instruct us from the rack. You are a rogue!' he screamed.

"The executioner who stood by asked that he be allowed to unloose me. When he commanded me to stand I could not move. He lifted me himself and suspended me by a rope, asking one of the bystanders to assist him in tying the hundred pound weight to my feet. All except the excutioner went away. 'Are you not a dumb fool, to think that God looks down to see what we are doing in this hole. That is ridiculous.' He said that unless I confessed they would not cease from racking me until my limbs should be rent asunder. The council returned, I cannot say after how long, and said that the lady of the castle had interceded for me; I should be tortured no longer."

Pieter had left the house and was standing beside a small linden tree, facing the river. The falling snow had covered his hat and clothing and the form they could see from the window looked like an elegant snowman. Occasionally Cecelia had asked the man to wait as she wrote. Her hand moved as a spindle, as if driven by a giant lantern wheel, her face expressionless, giving no sign that she even heard the words he said. Goris busied himself with the chores, feeding the fire, bringing water for tea. Occasionally he would go outside and stand silently beside Pieter for a few moments, then return to his duties. The two women sat on the bench where Goris and Pieter usually sat, sometimes holding hands, making no sound.

When Cecelia paused the man began speaking again, in the same unvaried and impassive fashion. "Three days later the lord returned with three priests, Calvinists, who disputed with and examined me. When they saw that their various disputations would not move me, that I would remain steadfast, one of them cried out, 'O you obdurate dog. We have tried all possible means and ways with you to convince you of your wrongdoing. If you would but suffer yourself to say two words you might go free.' I replied that the two words must be revealed by God and not themselves. They returned again the next day, that being Sunday, with more and new questions.

"When the priests and lord of the castle had gone one of the servants took me to a deep, dark, and filthy chamber, where I could see neither the sun nor the moon, so that I did not know when it was day or night, except when I could perceive that it was a little cooler and must be night outside. I was there for thirty-seven weeks they told me. I could not measure time for there was no light. It was so moist and damp in the chamber that my clothes rotted on my body, so that I became almost naked, and was without a single garment for a long time, only a coarse blanket they had given me which I wrapped around my body in the misery and darkness. My shirt had decayed to the point that only the collar remained, which I hung on the wall. The chamber had not been occupied for a long time and the vermin and loathsome reptiles were so numerous, eating my food if I so much as put it down, drowning in my drink until I found a stone to put on top of the pitcher. All of it caused me such terror that I feared total madness. At one time when these children of Pilate brought me out to try whether I would apostatize, the light so hurt my eyes that I was glad when they let me down again into the dungeon. And there was such a fetid stench which proceeded from the filth that was in this dark hole that no one could stay in my presence. When they brought me in even the councilors themselves could not question me but had to go away, saying they had never smelled such a horrible stench.

"But my chief affliction in this great trial was that I could get no tidings from the church or the brethren. At one time there was in the country a nobleman of Innsbruck, a lover of the Lord, who had a desire to hear some tidings from me. He sent word to the chamber by a friendly servant of the castle that if it were still well with me, if my heart still adhered firmly to God and his church, that I should send him a token: if I had nothing else, I should send him a little bit of straw, however little it might be. But such was the misery and poverty in which I sat that I could not even find that much in the chamber. Then I remembered the rotten collar which hung on the wall, a token which the servant took to his brother to say that I was still unchanged in my faith in God and in peace with the church. When the brother received the collar, and knew of my misery and poverty, he and his church felt great compassion for me, and after weeping bitterly and sorrowfully, they sent word back to me that they were very willing to send me clothes or anything else if I could receive it. But I knew that when such gifts were discovered they would throw me on the rack and torture me again, seeking the names of those who sent them. So I sent them word that the garment of patience would do me.

"When autumn and the frost were approaching they took me out to put me into another prison. There I had to stand, with one hand and one foot in the stocks, unable to lie or sit, only to stand, enduring such reproach and ridicule from the ungodly as 'There stands a holy man; nobody is as wise as he; there he stands as a light of the world.' And other such taunting remarks."

Cecelia raised her hand for him to stop. "Is there much more?" she asked. "The hour is late and I have not spoken with your companions. Perhaps you should return tomorrow."

"I can make it long or short," he said. "I know the flute in my voice must annoy you. It is from the rack. A stone was placed on my throat so that the pressure of it might choke me as I was being stretched by the ropes."

"Nothing annoys me," Cecelia said.

"Then I will tell the rest quickly," he said. "I will tell you quickly of how I summoned the actuary to me and witnessed to him that the judgment of God impelled him to do what he had done, that his heart was so hardened that there was nothing left for him but the heavy hand of God. About a fortnight afterwards he died very suddenly in the night, smitten with such fear that he cried and moaned terribly, lamenting that he had done a great wrong. I can tell you quickly of how the council decided to send me to the sea so that I should serve as a galley slave, to be stripped and scourged at the will of the captain. And of how the servant of the castle who was to deliver me to the sea became so drunk after we had left the castle—and we could not leave for five days after the council's decision because I had to learn to walk—that he rolled off the table which he thought was a bed. Seeing that he was not injured from the fall but continued to sleep, I unlatched the door of the house and left. And I must also tell you, if you can spare the time, that the lady of the castle called me to her before I left and promised never again to lay hands on one of the faithful and gave me money which I used for decent clothing when I returned to my father's house."

Pieter had returned and stood drying and thawing himself by the fire. Goris stood beside him, rubbing and patting the chills from his nape and shoulders. The two women and Jacob came and did the same, trying to put on a playful mood but with their presence sharing his burden. Pieter turned to Jacob and extended his hand, and they exchanged the kiss of peace. "Surely," Pieter said as he continued to hold the embrace, "you have experienced that the kingdom of heaven suffers violence and that the violent take it by force." Cecelia continued to sit as the scribe, consumed and obsessed.

Chapter Five

"ST. CECELIA, WOMAN of iron," Goris said as he entered the room.

"There are no saints," she said. "And if there are, God knows I'm not one of them. And the two of you must know by now that I am not of iron." She was writing from notes she had taken the previous evening, stopping only when she spoke.

"We know you are not iron," Goris replied, motioning with his head for her to stop writing. "But we're beginning to think you don't know it. You're burning yourself out, Cecelia." He placed his hand on the page, blocking the flow of the pen. "For two months you have done nothing but this. Every day. And every night. You don't even stop on Sunday. You sleep little. You seldom eat. You are losing weight and growing pale. When did you last go outside this house?"

"I don't remember. I think it was Christmas Eve. But never mind all that. Where is Pieter? And why have you brought no one to talk?"

"Pieter is walking the river. I saw him as I came but did not speak. I hear that they suspect he did not go to Antwerp as they assumed. They are searching for him."

"What else do you hear? What of the list? Tell me what they are doing about the list? The story must be finished before they come.

Tell me!" She pushed his hand away and stood up, her face red with anger.

"I don't know what they are doing about the list. I know they have it but that is all."

"How do you know they have it? Who told you they have the list? Are you keeping things from me, Goris? You must tell me everything. Now who told you they have the list?"

"You did," Goris said, his voice dropping, indicating with his hand that she could be heard outside. "You told me they have the list."

"Where is Pieter?" she asked again. "And why have you brought no one to talk?"

"I told you Pieter is exercising himself on the river. But he will not fall through if that is your worry." He pretended to tease. "The miller drove his team across it four days ago, bringing me flour. It has been frozen solid for five weeks. And I brought no one to talk because it is no fit night. It is the winter's worst storm. It was so cold in my shop the ovens could not be heated, but few people ventured outside so that I had no need of the bread anyway. I traded the butcher a part of what I had for meat. I brought it and thought we might have a feast. He says it is the best he will have until summer. Why don't you go to meet Pieter and I will prepare it. Then we can have a celebration. Enough of this work. We have done enough for now."

"We have done far too little," she said. "But please excuse my edginess. We will go together to the river. We will find Pieter and walk with him. Then we will prepare the meal together. The three of us together."

They walked through the drifts of snow which were continuing to build on the Amstel, sometimes climbing the dikes and strolling the empty streets. A full moon, hidden from view by the dense snow clouds, fused with the white meringue which blanketed all of the Low Countries, outlining every house and every tree in aspirated grace. Occasionally they stopped to play in the snow like children. They joined hands and pulled each other along the ice like sleds, staying close together, each drawing on the other for warmth and assurance.

Back inside the two men began to prepare the supper. Cecelia went immediately to the table and started to write.

"Why don't you let it be for tonight?" Goris called to her from the downstairs kitchen. "Why can't we enjoy ourselves, just cook and eat and drink wine? You said we would be together, now you leave us. Why can't we just play for once?"

"You and Pieter play house. But I'll not be as the Lutherans—standing with a New Testament in one hand and a beer mug in the other. She dropped the paper she was holding on the stair, picked it up and continued. "How do you think this sounds?" She began to read a line she had just written, moving halfway down the stairs so Pieter could hear. "The north wind of persecution blew now the more through the Garden of the Lord. With their brutish plans recessed by Boreas and his aids, they schemed to root the herbs and trees out of the earth through the violence they would inflict upon them when spring's sun again has its day." She had moved into the kitchen with them as she read. "Herbs and trees. Those are the true believers," she said when neither of them answered. They had both stopped what they were doing and stood looking at her. "Well, how did that sound as a chapter opening?" she asked them both.

"When will you stop, Cecelia?" Goris begged. "It is an unfit night, as I said. But I also brought no one here tonight so that you should rest. Instead you knead the bread even more fiercely. When will it end?"

"It will end when it ends," she answered, moving back up the stairs alone.

When they brought her food, a stew of lamb seasoned with mint, fresh bread, apples baked and glazed, she ate little, pushing the food about on the plate, drinking the tea in crude slurps, speaking as she did.

"I am writing now of Maeyken Wens. Remember the story? I have my notes here. Hendrix Toe Water recounted it to us. Remember? She was such a faithful and persistent witness, admonishing the council even as they sentenced her to death by fire; before they led her to the stake the executioner latched her tongue to the roof of her mouth with a screw, so that she could not give audible praise to the Lord. Her two sons, one fifteen and one four years old, came to be with their mother as she died, the younger one falling into a dead faint as he saw them shove the ladder upon which she was bound onto the fire. I have written here of how these two little ones searched the ashes of the fire next day to find the tongue screw, their only remembrance of their dear mother, all her possessions having been confiscated for the benefit of the Imperial Majesty." She spoke with sundered rhythm, gasping a breath with each quick pause.

Pieter and Goris sat listening, gazing into the fire, helpless to divert her. At first it had been a sort of game with them, running her errands, gathering materials she asked for, bringing the visitors to her door, but now as they watched her dwindling body, dedicated with such fierce loyalty to her purpose, driven and possessed by an unknown spirit, they wondered if their devotion had not been misguided. She took no interest anymore in the orderliness of the house and neglected her own hygiene and appearance. If they were not with her when night came they would find her straining with her pen in the darkness, not bothering to trim the lamp or light a candle. And twice they found her shivering in the cold, the fire dead, not even aware that she was freezing.

"Do you think it is fear that drives her so?" Goris asked as they worked to put the kitchen in order.

"Fear of what?" Pieter asked. "Of death? All of us know that before the poppies raise their heads again they will come for us. That is, unless we escape."

"Escape?" Goris said, blinking as if the thought would not register. "Escape," he said again, not as a question now. "What is it that drives her so?"

"I do not believe it is fear of death," Pieter said. "But it is fear of something."

Cecelia called to them from the landing. "What keeps you so long! The holiday is over. The feast is finished. Why will you not return to work!" There was the same harshness in her voice that Goris had heard earlier.

"We're playing chambermaid," Goris said. "We're cleaning your kitchen."

"Never mind your chambering," she said. "I need you here."

They left what they were doing and climbed the stairs. "Have you forgotten that I asked you days ago to find for me the exact wording of a judge's sentence. May I assume that you have it for me? I have a place to use it now." She was speaking to Pieter but Goris replied.

"I have the wording. It was out of the question for Pieter to go in search of it. I promised to find it. I have a shopper who works for the Council. He was once a witness at a trial and copied the judge's words. It is at the shop. I will bring it tomorrow."

"Will you bring it now?" she asked, her voice rising with impatience.

"Now?" Pieter said. "You will send him unto this storm for a bit of paper?"

Goris had already started to leave. "There will be worse storms to come," she said, watching him out the door.

Neither Pieter nor Cecelia spoke while Goris was gone. She continued to write and Pieter sat watching her. Once he started to return to the kitchen, thought better of it, and remained seated.

"It is in German," Goris said when he returned, handing the paper to Pieter.

Pieter began to read but Cecelia interrupted. "Will you wait until I am ready? I am in the midst of a thought." Pieter shrugged and winked at Goris, motioning for him to sit beside him on the bench.

"Now," Cecelia said, almost before Goris was seated. "But please translate slowly. I want to get it correct." Pieter began to read, stopping when he finished each line until she nodded for him to continue.

> Whereas Ryer Dircks, boatman, citizen of this city, did about three years ago, embrace the doctrines, errors, sects, and heresies of the Anabaptists, and in holding pernicious views with regard to the sacraments of the holy church, contrary to the holy Christian faith, the ordinances of the holy church, and the written laws and decrees of his Imperial Majesty, our gracious lord, and, moreover, persists in his errors and heresies, notwithstanding the instruction given him in the true faith; therefore, my lords of the court, having heard the demand made by my lord the bailiff, in the name of his Imperial Majesty, concerning the aforementioned Ryer Dircks, as also his confession, and having duly considered the circumstan-

> ces of the case, condemn said Ryer Dircks, pursuant to the aforesaid decrees, to be executed in the following manner: To have his hands bound with string before him. To have his knees lifted between his bound wrists, and to have a stick thrust between the bound wrists and his calves. In this secure position to be placed on a wagon, gagged so that he may not further speak, and taken through the streets so that all may see. To be taken to the Amstel and placed by the executioner in a boat. To be pushed into the river by the executioner and drowned. And, furthermore, his property to be confiscated for the benefit of his Imperial Majesty, as Count of Holland, without derogation and prejudice to the privileges of this city. Thus pronounced, and committed to the executioner for execution, this sixteenth day of August, A.D. 1548, in the presence of the bailiff, all the burgomasters, and all the judges, with the exception of Jan Dunen.

"Is that all?" Cecelia asked after she had completed copying the last line he had read.

"Is it not enough?" Goris said, seeing none of the revulsion in Cecelia's face that he felt within himself.

"It is not enough," Cecelia answered. "It is not enough for they did not record the true reason for his execution. They make no mention of community of goods. That is why they hate us so, we agreed. You must find another example of a sentence. One in which they admit what they fear most from us."

"Is it something more gory you wish?" Pieter asked, searching for words to alter the tension which seemed to increase with each exchange. "Here. Here's a sentence for you. You gave it to me yourself. Listen. 'In the case of the Governor of his Imperial Majesty versus Michael Sattler, judgment is passed, that Michael Sattler shall be delivered to the executioner, who shall lead him to the place of execution, and cut out his tongue; then throw him upon a wagon, and there tear his body twice with red hot tongs; and after he has been brought without the gate, he shall be pinched five times in the same manner, his head placed upon a stick as an example for the heretics, and his body quartered and placed upon a wheel as food for birds and beasts.' There. Is that picture enough for your precious story? If it is blood you seek for your parchment then we can spread it upon every page.

"And, here. Here's another one," he said. "This sentence pronounced upon thirty-six at once. 'According to justice for these sectarians, because of their evil designs, their hearts are to be cut out, while alive, and thrown into their faces; their bodies quartered, and hung upon the town gates, and their heads placed on stakes.' Surely that one will suit you!" The clinical stance he had taken in the beginning was soon lost in his own ranting. He moved in circles around the table, Goris following, trying to calm him.

Cecelia did not move from where she sat. She did not look up from her writing and did not raise her voice as she spoke. "It is not theatre, my brothers, that I seek. It is the story. You asked what it is that I fear. I heard your words to each other. I fear that we will be recorded as a minor nuisance, a flea wrestling with a bear, a comic interlude in what they call the great Lutheran struggle for freedom. Or not recorded at all. Awake, my brother! If it is time to preach to each other, then hear my sermon. Everywhere we are hated and feared and hunted down like rabbits by processions of armed horsemen. The peaceful marshes of the Ems where our brethren seek refuge have been turned into moors of carnage. From Flanders to Danzig. From Paris to the Tyrol and from Moravia to Amsterdam it is the same. Even the mighty fortressed Luther lumped us with peasant revolutionaries and boasted that mouths such as ours can best be answered with a fist that brings sweat from the nose, that our ears must be unbuttoned with bullets till our heads jump off our shoulders, and exhorted his votaries to hew, stab, slay, to smite us all as mad dogs secretly or openly. They call our courage despair. Our pitiful huts hidden among the buckwheat fields and fir trees yield quickly to the torch of tyranny. Our communities become pyres, lacking even an accuser. While the reformers' principles are enforced with the swords of the princes, our principles are cut down by the same princes at the behest of the reformers. I do not think that our telling of the story will save us from the world. But I think it will let the world know that we were here."

She had placed the quill in the well and pushed it to the end of the table. Pieter and Goris sat watching her, both of them calm now. The long silence was strangely comfortable. It was Goris who broke it with words which surprised Pieter. "And what else are you afraid of, Cecelia?" His voice was gentle but assertive.

It was as if it had been asked on cue, that Cecelia knew that it would be asked and was waiting with her answer.

"Very well," she sighed. "I will tell you." But then she started to cry. At first it was just a whimper, a sort of mewing, like the sound of newborn kittens. She fought to stifle it, the muscles in her neck moving like one trying to swallow too much at once, but then she dropped her head upon the table and fell into convulsive, almost hysterical wailing.

Pieter moved to go to her, but Goris placed his hand on his knee. "Let her be." Her body shook and she made no effort now to contain the sounds. They had not seen her cry like this before and for a time they watched her more out of curiosity than sympathy. But then the two of them began to weep also, first Pieter, then Goris, the tears streaming down their faces, neither attempting to conceal or wipe them away. With no one leading they moved to the center of the room and stood together as one person, their sobs forming one sound, like close harmony, singing.

When the crying stopped, as abruptly as it had begun, they moved back to their places as if it had not happened at all, Cecelia at the table, Goris and Pieter seated on the same bench.

"Then tell us," Goris said, his voice the same as before.

"I have been frightened since Jacob Cool described the rack to us," she began, seeming not to be embarrassed by what she was about to tell them. "Of course, all of us have known the torture, the wheels, funnels, thumb and tongue screws, all of it. But there is something I had never thought of before. I have been prepared for the pain, the stretching, the beating, all the rest. Even death which I know will come. None of it would make me deny the faith I hold. But there is one thing which I fear I cannot withstand." She spoke now with no show of emotion. And no awkwardness.

"You recall what Anna told us, about their putting the screws to her shins? And the ropes about her thighs?" She paused for at least a minute, staring at first one and then the other, before continuing. "No man has ever touched my bare body. I am not sure that I can stand to be dishonored. If they will but permit me to leave the world with dignity, I will go gladly. But if I must be defiled, if my naked body must suffer the stares of strangers, if I am to be fondled by the lewd and wanton hands of a pagan bailiff. . . ." She was close to crying again but Goris interrupted. Pieter's great learning had not prepared him for what he was hearing and he was relieved that Goris was not struck dumb as he was.

"Wait a minute," Goris said, slowly but sharply. "Your fears are exaggerated by your modesty. Remember also that the Procurator General, when Anna protested a similar happening . . . do you forget what he said? It is their understanding of morality, of honor. When Anna said that she had never been touched, he said, 'Miss Anna, we shall not treat you dishonorably.' The Procurator seemed hurt that she would suspect him. To me it makes no sense, but that is what he told her. We do not enter this world with dignity," Goris added. "Why expect to leave it that way?"

"I know. I know," Cecelia said. "But that makes my fear no less."

Goris started to speak again, but Cecelia motioned him to silence. "You are kind to console me, Goris, and I do not expect you to understand. You are generous not to laugh. I know that it makes no sense. But I have lived alone all these years. Before that only with my father. I am not experienced in such matters. I remember what Anna said. I remember also the account Felix told us of poor Margaret, how, as she was being led to the scaffold the executioner had unlaced her gown, so that when she ascended the scaffold it fell down, leaving her standing there in her shift and linen pants which he had made her put on by way of mockery. So ashamed was she that she hastened to the stake so that her shame might be quickly ended by the flames.

"And also the three sisters in Antwerp, after being drowned in a barrel in prison, thrown shamefully naked into the Scheldt."

"But they shall be clothed," Pieter said. It was the first time he had spoken.

"I have no doubt of it," she said. "My doubts are of myself, not of God."

"Then why don't we escape?" Pieter said, matter of factly. "Why don't we leave Amsterdam?" He spoke as if he referred to some holiday journey. Cecelia did not seem surprised by what he said.

"To where?" she asked, indicating no resistance to the thought.

"To many places. To northwest Germany. There are many of our refugees there. I know where they are. We could be farmers. We can build a hut in one of the established settlements. I can. . . ."

"Pieter. Pieter. Poor, poor Pieter. None of us is a farmer. You are a printer. Goris can survive as a baker and nothing more. And no one is going to pay me to teach them Latin."

"Then we can go to Marburg. To Zurich. To Tyrol. There are many places we might go. To Britain. I have sent some of our refugees there already. We will go west. To the new country. We can sign as merchant seamen, dress you up, disguise you, and lose ourselves when we get there. There are many Dutch there already and no doubt some of them are of the faith. We can. . . ."

"Pieter. Pieter. Dear Pieter," Cecelia said again. "You are dreaming. What pity and what kindness you have within you, but I will not leave my story. I will not leave my home, my father's house. I am not scum. I am of noble origin and state. We know they have the list. And we know they will come for us. You know of my fear, my burden. But God will give me strength. If I must suffer the foul injury of defilement, I will pray that he will close my mouth and make me strong. No, I will not pray to be strong. I will pray to be weak, so weak that I swoon at their first offense against me. For when I am weak, then am I strong. The holy Apostle said it. And knowing that, we take pleasure in infirmities, in reproaches, in necessities, in persecutions, in distresses. I will not recant."

"Then I will recant," Pieter said. He said it with no passion at all.

"You will recant?" Goris said, astonished and confused.

"Yes, I will recant."

"Of what?" Cecelia said, not showing the bewilderment Goris had expressed.

"For you," Pieter said.

"I did not ask 'for whom?' I asked 'for what?' You will recant for me?" she added, understanding what he meant. She spoke as one touched by such incredible joy that she dared not acknowledge it.

"So that I might not be dishonored you will recant?" she said, rising and moving about the room. "Such friendship must surely lie beyond the ambit of grace. But though I should be gnawed by the waterrats of a thousand dungeons, my person violated by the most barbarous creature, and my naked remains hurled ignominiously upon my father's grave, I could not have it." She crossed the room, opened one of the shutters enough to peer into the darkness, then closed it quickly and turned around, shaking her head slowly. "Do you know what you say? That you could commit your own soul to hell in defense of my foolish modesty? Surely, Goris, our brother has lost his senses." Goris did not answer.

"It is not foolish modesty." Pieter said, moving toward her. "And I have not lost my senses. Do you think that God does not know of pardon? Of mercy? Do we suppose that grace is an attribute of man alone? Did we not agree that our salvation is of the faithfulness of God?"

"Then I must ask again," Goris said. "How are we different from the others?"

"Different?" Pieter asked. "We are not trying to be different. We are trying to be faithful servants. Slaves! If I go to the depths of hell for recanting before God's enemies, then so be it. And remember what Jacob Cool told us? 'The telling of the story is not the story.' I am not the story. I am a part of the telling of the story. Nothing more. Nothing!"

"You are a man of learning, of logic," Goris said, his voice rising. "I am a dumb baker. But it appears to me that you are walking the river on thin ice."

"Perhaps so," Pieter said, still calm. "But even if I send my soul to hell, perhaps the ice is not so thin as you believe. What greater love can I have for Jesus, what greater honor than to risk sending my own soul to hell for His sake. If I treasure my own soul more than Him... do not even the Publicans the same?"

"But you are not risking it for His sake," Cecelia interrupted. "You are risking it for my sake."

But you . . . we are His little ones," Pieter said. "Inasmuch . . . but enough of this. Listen to me. I have seen how they work. I know of their transmutation of sentences. They will agree to anything to prove the weakness of one of us. I am not pleading for anyone's safety. Not even my own. They will torture me first because I have been their prisoner before. They will want to know where I have been, who I have taught, if I have baptized anyone. I will tell them none of that. When they have tormented me sufficiently, just when they believe that I am on the verge of confessing, I will ask that the council be brought. Then I will offer to recant if they agree to end your life without defilement. And they will accept the proposal. They will do anything for one recantation."

He pushed the papers aside and stretched himself out on the table, pretending that he was lying on the rack, and began to speak. Goris and Cecelia stood on each side, listening and watching closely.

> "My lords, the council. I know that soon you will ask me again to denounce my faith. If I do so, you will set me free. But if I denounce my faith here in this prison, in the presence of these few, you will have gained little. I offer you now a proposal I think you cannot refuse."

Pieter struggled feebly on the table, then lay quiet as if waiting for a response from his tormentors. After a long pause he continued.

> "If you will agree in the presence of all the burgomasters to the sentence I offer for Sister Cecelia Geronymus, then I will recant and denounce my faith. Not at this moment with only you to hear it, but at the time of my death when it will be witnessed by many. Believers and unbelievers together."

He stopped again, his body trembling slightly. Cecelia was breathing rapidly and deeply, sighing softly with each outward breath. Goris had moved to her side of the table and stood with his hand on her shoulder. Pieter's eyes were glazed as he lay on the table and he did not appear to see them. When he spoke again his voice was deep and resonant and deliberate, the tone and manner of a judge. He seemed detached from it all as he recited the proposed sentence for Cecelia.

> "In the case of the Governor of his Imperial Majesty versus Cecelia Geronymus, a native of Amsterdam, who has confessed to teaching against the baptism administered to her at her birth, who has attended certain conventicles in which pernicious views with regard to the holy sacrament of the altar, all of which is contrary to the ordinances and the faith of the holy Church of his Imperial Majesty, and also contrary to the

written laws and decrees of our gracious lord, as count of Holland, were taught, who obstinately persists in her beliefs and who admits that she has practiced community of goods contrary to the decrees of his Imperial Majesty, having duly regarded the circumstances of the case, having heard the demand made by my lord the bailiff concerning the aforesaid Cecelia Geronymus, condemn said Cecelia Geronymus to be executed in the following manner:
To be delivered to the executioner without torture, and that she be placed in a bag, fully clothed in a manner of her usual attire, and that a rope be tied to the boat of the executioner, that her body be lowered gently by the executioner and that she remain in the water of the Amstel until she be drowned, her corpse then to be delivered to her survivors for burial according to her own prescribed ritual."

When he finished reciting the sentence which he would ask the judge to impose upon Cecelia, he continued to lie on the table. His body was trembling convulsively now. Muscles and tendons in his legs, arms, and chest jerked and vibrated. His cheeks and lips quivered and a low gurgling sound came from his throat. Goris and Cecelia did not move. They watched him the way one watches at a death bed, when there is nothing left to say or do except stay until the end. Goris held Cecelia tightly around her waist, occasionally nestling his head upon her shoulder where his hand had been earlier, like a frightened child would do. Cecelia stood with magnificent poise, fixed as a marble statue, oblivious to everything except the words she was hearing. The heavy breathing and sighing were gone.

When Pieter slid from the table he had trouble moving about the room. He almost fell to the floor as he struggled to maintain his balance. The film over his eyes did not go away, and as he stumbled to and fro, he looked the way he had when he came to Cecelia's house three months earlier, before they began the project. Goris followed, slightly behind him, sometimes supporting him, sometimes encouraging him along with his gentle words. When he regained his composure and came to rest at last against the huge mantel ledge, he cleared his throat loudly, shook his head in quick jerks like one trying to recover from a deep trance, and began to speak in his normal manner.

"You see, I will ask for no relief from my own bonds. I do not ask to be strangled before I reach the fire, though death is quicker that way. I will not ask for the gunpowder upon my person as others often do so that the fire will be more swift in ending it all. If they will grant this sentence to you, my sister, my love . . . I will denounce the faith . . . as I die . . . with no prayer to God for my forgiveness."

"But . . . but . . . but," Goris interrupted, prancing around the room, his hands flailing the air. "Are you saying you will curse God Almighty at the very moment of your death? Brother . . . my . . . sister . . . Cecelia . . . Pieter . . . I must be a more thick-witted baker than ever I supposed."

"You are not thick-witted, my brother," Pieter said, calmer still. "And our faith is not measured in terms of our learning. So tell me, what greater love can I show our Lord than to be willing to go to hell for His sake?"

Goris turned to face Cecelia who continued to stand mute, overwhelmed but restored, her countenance as lucent as an autumn moon. His gaze pleaded for her intervention. But she did not move.

Pieter again stretched his long, bony frame upon the table, assuming the same position he had before, and began to speak. "My lord the executioner, and any judges and my lords the council. It is the moment of my death. I desire to reclaim the baptism given to me at my birth. At this moment of my death I renounce the rites and ordinances practiced by me among the Anabaptists."

When he climbed down from the table this time he was quick and steady. He spoke directly to Goris, spoke as if Cecelia were not even in the room. "That, my brother, is what I will say before I die if the sentence I have proposed be pronounced upon our sister."

As Goris and Pieter continued to talk heatedly, Cecelia took a large linen towel from the cupboard and tied it about her waist. When they sat down together on the bench she poured water from an earthen pitcher into a basin. Kneeling down before them she removed their shoes, no one speaking a word now. Instead of washing the feet of one and then moving to the other she took Pieter's left foot and Goris's right in her hands together, dipped them together into the basin, and bathed them as if they were one foot. She dried them in the same fashion, dabbing at first with the linen towel, then taking them both together as one, she wrapped them inside the towel, fretting over each toe, squeezing and patting the two feet as one until they were dry. When she finished, she motioned for them to change places and washed the other feet the same way. When she was done, still with no one speaking, they stood up. When she sat down, they knelt before her as she had knelt before them. As they washed her feet, both of them bathing each foot, they began to sing, Cecelia joining in:

I call to thee, my God, my king.
    Strengthen my faith.
O Christ, my humble friend,
    Wash me in thy grace.

Chapter Six

GORIS HAD WANTED to tell them earlier of the rumors of the streets, the things he had heard in his shop from those who were friendly, but Cecelia had decided that the story should be told in two languages. So for more than a month he had watched them as they worked, correcting, adding to, deleting from what was written. As she read aloud Pieter translated and copied her Dutch words into German. Sometimes they worked through the night, stopping only when one of them fell asleep at the table. As they did their work, Goris dozed beside the fire, jumping up at the slightest hint of a need. He had continued to work in the shop, the only income they had. He also prepared the meals, ran the errands, supervised the house, quietly closing the door of each day as it passed. When there was time and it seemed appropriate to him, he sat with them, listening, making suggestions when something was not clear to him. And more than they, he waited.

"Where's the church?" he asked from where he lay on the floor, not even opening his eyes.

"The Church is here," Cecelia said, answering in the same casual tone as he had asked the question. She turned immediately back to the paper in her hand, reading a sentence to Pieter.

"Why here?" Goris asked, still not opening his eyes.

"Where two or three are gathered," Cecelia said. She glanced down at him and then quickly read another sentence.

Goris pulled himself up onto one elbow. "What about one?" he asked.

"One what?" Cecelia said, looking impatiently at him as he shifted his weight to the other elbow.

"One person. You said where two or three are gathered. Why not one?"

"One person cannot be the church," she said. She whispered and smiled, like one trying to quiet an inquiring child's questions.

"Why?"

"Just because," she said, growing more impatient now.

"Because what?" he said.

"Because the Book says where two or three are *gathered*. One person cannot gather." She had put the sheet down and was looking at Pieter, seeking his aid in quieting Goris.

"It takes two or three to gather, Goris," Pieter said, humoring him, continuing to copy the last sentence she had read.

"What about four?" Goris said. "What about where four or five are gathered?"

"I don't know," she said, whispering and smiling again. "Jesus just said two or three. I assume He meant at least two or three. It could be more."

"Then why didn't He say that?" Goris said, sitting upright, an itch in his own voice now. "Why do we think Jesus didn't say just exactly what He meant? We're falling into the same trap as the priests. Always having to say that He meant more, or meant less than what He actually said. Was He not fully as smart as they? Or as we?"

"Are you being frivolous, Goris?" Cecelia asked, less sure of her ground now.

"I think he is not being frivolous," Pieter said, putting his quill in the well and walking over beside him.

"I am not being frivolous. I think two or three. But not four or five."

"Why?" Cecelia asked, trying to mimic Goris at first, then

quickly asking it in her own voice. "Why?"

"Because when there are more than two or three they start looking for a leader. He's in the midst of two or three but not four or five or eight hundred."

"Perhaps not. Perhaps so," Cecelia said, speaking sharply again. Then adding, "That's a nice lesson, Goris. Now, will you let us get back to the story?" Pieter had returned to his seat at the table.

Goris stood up, walked to the table and sat down between them. He placed one hand on the stack of parchment in front of Cecelia, reached over and placed the other one on the stack before Pieter, his palms turned upward. They sat looking at the big hands, big enough to cover the sheets without spreading his fingers, hands clean and strong and supple from the years of practicing his trade. Neither of them spoke.

"No, my sister. My brother. But it is not I who will not let you get back to the story. Our story is done. They are coming for us tomorrow." He said it without affect, as if reporting some minor event of the city.

Without a word Cecelia left the room and started down the stairs. Pieter moved to go after her but Goris placed his hand on his knee. "Let her be."

"Do you know this for sure?" Pieter asked when she was out of sight.

"Wait until she returns," Goris said. "We will be what we are. We are three. Three gathered have no secrets."

"But I have a secret," Pieter said. "She had her secret and I have mine, and you had yours. You have known that they were coming."

"Then tell it to me now," Goris said. "Tell me your secret before she returns."

"I am afraid. I have fear."

"What is your fear? Tell it to me before Cecelia returns."

"I had hoped the cup would pass. Now that hope is gone."

"Then you have no fear," Goris said, gesturing through the window with his hand.

"But I do," Pieter said, leaning to stare him directly in the face.

"You cannot have it both ways, my brother," Goris said. "It

makes no sense to fear without hope. Fear is lost when hope is lost. You may have fear if you still have hope. But if you have no hope you can have no fear."

"Well, of course, I have hope in the perfect love of God. But that is not what I mean."

"First John, four, eighteen," Goris said, gesturing to the big Lutheran Bible on the cupboard. "Look it up."

Pieter moved across the room, taking one of the candles with him to the cupboard. He opened the Bible and turned the pages until he found the passage. He read it to himself in German, recited it under his breath in French. Then he turned to Goris and said it aloud in Dutch. "There is no fear in love, for perfect love casteth out fear." He closed the book but continued to stand beside the cupboard. "She taught you to read well, didn't she?" he said.

"Yes," Goris said. "She taught me to read well."

They sat on the bench together, gazing into the fire but saying nothing until Cecelia came back.

"Do you know this for sure?" she said, sitting on the bench between them. She was dressed as they had never seen her before. She was wearing a heavy gray kirtle, full length, with sleeves tied about her wrists. A high collar, made of the same material but separate from the rest of the garment, covered her neck and was held in place, directly under her chin, by a plain silver pin. A white linen apron, reaching almost to her ankles, was tied tightly about her waist. A knitted bonnet of coarse black wool with a light shawl attached covered her head and fell over her shoulders like a tippet. Her shoes, black leather with slight heels, were hooked above the ankles; not even the black stockings underneath were showing. Her brown hair, washed and brushed to a lustrous hue, a tinge of red glistening in the light of the candle behind her, fell straight down her back, unbraided. As she entered the room the smell of soft cleanness followed as she strolled.

"Yes," Goris said. "I know it for sure. They have the list and the bailiff has given sanction to fifty armed horsemen to find everyone on the list. But he will come for us himself. He knows that Pieter is here. And he knows about the project. It is my fault. Someone I brought for the interview was not of us."

"Where two or three are gathered they do not apologize," Cecelia said. "It is not a matter of fault."

Cecelia stood up and began to move about the house. With a feather duster she cleaned the furniture, wiping each chair, bench, table and cupboard with a piece of broadcloth when she had dusted it. She folded bedsheets, handcloths, two tablecloths, and a dozen table napkins, all made of linen, and placed them in a neat stack on top of a large oak chest. All the blankets, except those on the beds, were stacked on an eight-sided table beside the chest.

"These must be distributed before they come," Cecelia said.

"Blaisus knows they are coming. I told him you would leave them in the peat closet. He will get them later."

"That will not do," Cecelia said. "The sentence will call for the confiscation of all my possessions. If I give them away before they come they are no longer my possessions. To do it later would be to steal what already belongs to them."

"They will remain your possessions until after the sentencing," Goris said. "Not even the Anabaptists are guilty until the judges give the word. Blaisus will distribute it all properly."

She moved into other parts of the house. Silver buttons, a few ornaments of gold—earrings, hair brooches, a medallion and chain—were placed in a small basket. A few pieces of decorative porcelain and several buckles, beakers, and head ornaments were added.

She walked about straightening and dusting several paintings hanging on the walls. "It would be risky for Blaisus to place these on the market," she said. "The curtains and fireplace coverings had best stay as well."

After the things she had collected were placed in the peat closet she walked through the house again, making sure that each room was orderly. When she had finished she reached in the cupboard and got the decanter containing the wine which had been poured for Gillis the night the project had begun. She placed it in the center of the table.

"Does that mean you have forgiven him?" Goris asked.

"For betraying us?" she asked.

"No," Goris said. She looked at him but did not answer.

She came and sat by the fire and began to talk. "What power do they have over us? Even as they come for us they see us because God has trimmed the wick of His lamp to light the day. The rivers and canals are melted not by their bidding. But ours is not the first innocent blood to stain the streets of Amsterdam, nor to breathe our last in Amstel's waters. So let them act according to their laws. Surely it is better to die innocent than guilty."

"But we are guilty," Goris said. "We have done all the things they will charge. And more."

"But they are not wrong things," Cecelia said. "Our hearts are pure before God."

"But it is not God who will kill us. When the tormentors set their minds, the sword falls, the flames leap up, the waters fill our bellies. It does not have to do with purity of heart. It has to do with offense to their laws. And of that we cannot plead innocence. We will not baptize our young, punishable by death since Justinius. We will not swear. We will not bear the sword for them . . . and we share our goods. Community of goods—I think you are right. From the talk I hear, it is for that that they hate us most."

"But we do not really do that," Pieter said. "We are not really *der Kommunists*. You said so yourself."

"But they believe we are communist," Goris said. "And that is enough. If they think we are seditious, we are seditious. That is what sedition is. It is what they say it is, what they think it is. The bread is risen when it is risen, but it is baked when I say it is risen. The dough is not lord of the baker. The baker is lord of the loaf."

Cecelia fell into a spell of deep sighing. At first it was nothing more than heavy breathing, her shoulders and breasts heaving and falling with no sound. But suddenly the room was filled with the gripping sounds of lamentation and distress. "Ohhohohoho. Ohhohohoho." Goris and Pieter were making the same sounds as Cecelia. Between the thrusts of shouts and sobs there could be heard some brief recitation from one or the other of them. "For our light affliction, which is but for a moment, worketh for us a far more exceeding and eternal weight of glory." Then all together again, gutteral moans of unutterable hurt. "There shall be no death, neither sorrow nor crying, neither shall there be any more pain, for the former things are passed away. Ohuhuhuhuhu. If God be for us, who can be against us?" Then more agonizing screams of anguish. For a time they were simply milling about the room aimlessly, sighing, moaning, each one making their individual noises of passion.

Cecelia lifted her hands and head and voice toward the ceiling and called out, "Let the sighing of the prisoner come before thee." Goris followed with the same motions and called out, "According to the Greatness of thy power." Pieter did the same, adding, "Preserve thou those who are appointed to die."

They formed a circle and with their hands still lifted, repeated the words in unison: "Let the sighing of the prisoner come before thee; according to the greatness of thy power preserve thou those who are appointed to die."

The lamentation moved abruptly and without interruption into sounds of joy and exultation and celebration. They embraced and patted each other and spoke congratulatory words, dancing, laughing more loudly than they had wept. For more than an hour they sang and frolicked about the room, sometimes playing follow the leader as they pranced through the house, up and down the stairs, twice sliding down the banister, crawling under the table on hands and knees as if it were a tunnel. Sometimes they joined hands and skipped in a circle like children, moving first in one direction and then the other.

"Let's go visiting," Cecelia said, getting their coats from the hall, not even waiting for them to reply. Goris and Pieter followed her into the night without question. They stopped for a few minutes beside Harlaan's tannery, a place they had often gathered for their meetings.

"Shall we awaken him?" Pieter asked.

"No," Cecelia said. "We shall see him soon enough. He needs his rest."

When they reached Goris's shop he unlatched the door and they followed him inside. He checked the ovens as he had done each night for twenty years. It was plain that he had not baked for several days. The ashes in the furnace were cold and white. With Pieter's help he shoveled them clean, emptying the ashes in a pit behind his living quarters. Cecelia took the few remaining loaves and placed them on the ledges facing the street. "Let the stray dogs eat," she said to herself, putting two loaves on the lower ledge. "And this is for whomever takes them." She stacked the other loaves on the higher shelf.

Goris chuckled when he saw what she had done. "Something for the bailiff?" he asked.

"Maybe," she said. "Bailiffs eat too."

"Yes, I suppose they do. 'Inasmuch as ye have done it unto the least of these.' Caesar's bailiff must surely be the least. Until now that passage had always given me trouble."

"Through a glass, darkly. Now face to face," Cecelia said, looking into the night, not talking to Goris.

Pieter and Cecelia watched as Goris placed his simple possessions in order. He took two stalks of barley from underneath the counter where he displayed his bread and laced them into a wreath shape. "I saved them from my first baking," he said. He opened the door to the second oven and peered inside for a moment. "The bread is rising," he whispered.

Pieter turned his good ear to Cecelia and asked what he had said. She cupped her hand to his ear and said, "He said the resurrection is certain." Pieter did not answer.

Back in his living quarters he took a flat package from a large trunk and unwrapped it. He held up a faded painting in a silver frame, oval shaped with small blossoms embossed around the edges. He held it near the candle and the two of them moved to see it clearly. It was of a young woman, very dark, with fine black hair captured in two buns on either side of her head. The painting itself was of poor quality but the natural beauty of her countenance showed through. "My father did it," he said. He wiped it clean and placed it on a mantel near his bed. "It was after they were married," he said, looking at it again before he walked away.

The clock in the tower of St. Nicolas Church struck three o'clock. They moved in the direction of the sound. No one spoke when they reached the arc leading into the well-kept churchyard. They stood close together, looking at the very tip of the spires silhouetted against low hanging clouds, clouds which at times seemed to smother the steeple itself, hiding it from view almost completely. "Do you want to go in?" Cecelia asked.

"Do you?" Pieter said.

"It used to be so beautiful," Cecelia said, moving away, neither answering the question of the other.

"It is too big to be beautiful," Goris said.

They paused in front of shops and stores as they walked. "That was my father's business," Cecelia said, pointing to an upstairs office. "And there is where we were baptized. I wonder where old Gillis, the baptizer, is tonight. He dipped water from the well with a gourd."

"If he had waited one month there would have been plenty of water," Goris said. "But leave the gourd for Jonah."

"Yes, I remember that flood. We even got blamed for that," Cecelia said. "They said it was heresy that brought the strong northwest wind during high tides. I remember the dikes breaking on this very spot, the waters rushing in on every side, rolling with resistless fury, sweeping houses, trees, men, and cattle in its wake."

They stopped beside the canal where Goris had his boat moored. "You have served me well," he said, pulling the boat through the slushy ice which broke in pieces as he pulled it to him. When he had removed all the lines he pushed it away with his boot. "Don't stop until you float to Emden," he said, watching the retreating tide pull it away. "Someone there will treat you well."

"What will ever become of our Netherlands?" Goris said as they began walking in the direction of Cecelia's house. "Will she ever blush for what is happening to us now?"

"She is no worse than the others," Cecelia said. "The lowering clouds of despotism and superstition hang dark over all of Europe today. Scenes of violence, of bloodshed and oppression are rampant everywhere. That's the story we have written. But a land which gave us an Erasmus will one day grant us liberty. And when that meridian splendor makes its rounds it will light the way for all the world. Whatever the private interests of the princes, one day they will be a rare occurrence, and the fear they engender will be no more. A people who could snatch this ground from the sea will not let it be forever ruled by tyranny and falsehood. The blood of some may be in vain, but the red blood of Holland's martyrs will paint the corners of the earth. I would die for my Lord anywhere, but I am happy that He will let me die in Amsterdam." They had not heard her speak this way before; neither of them answered.

It was almost dawn when they climbed the stairs to the room where they had written the book. Cecelia put two small pieces of wood on the fire and blew on it until the coals flamed up. She walked to the table and picked up the thick manuscript Pieter had translated to German and handed it to him. She took the Dutch version, written in her own elegant hand, and sat on the bench facing the fire.

She began to pray aloud, looking straight ahead, not bowing her head and not closing her eyes. "Grace, joy, and peace from God the heavenly Father, and our Lord Jesus Christ, who loved us, and washed us from our sins in His own blood, and hath shined bright in our hearts, and translated us into Goris and Pieter and Cecelia in Amsterdam. We thank thee for the story. We thank thee for the Church of two or three gathered, for the assurance that whosoever loseth his life for thy sake and the Gospel's the same shall find it hereafter in life eternal. We thank thee for the words of our brother Paul who said, 'Whatsoever things were written aforetime were written for our learning.' And let us not fear men, which must perish like grass; but let us fear God, whose story shall abide forever."

She moved from where she sat and stood directly behind Goris and Pieter, holding her right hand over their heads, still holding the manuscript in the other. "Herewith I commend you to the Lord, and to the story of His grace. May He comfort, strengthen, stablish you all with His Spirit, that you may finish that whereunto you are called, to the praise and glory of the Lord, so that we may rejoice together, and sit down at the Lord's table, where He shall serve us with new wine, in the kingdom of God, His father."

She did not say Amen when she stopped but took her place again on the bench. She turned the stack of paper face side down, so that the last page she had written was on the top, the writing away from her. She motioned for Pieter to do the same. Taking the top page, the last words she had written, she leaned forward and dropped it quickly into the flame. "Jacob Cool was right," she whispered. "May he and God the Father forgive me for my sin. Writing the story is not the *Story*."

"Is it what you wish?" Pieter asked, watching the flame of the parchment as it filled the room with light, not dropping the sheet he held.

"Is it what I wish? No. It is not what I wish," she said, adding, "*Thy* kingdom come. *Thy* will be done," then pausing as she watched Pieter hold the end of the sheet in the fire, holding it until the flame was almost to his fingertips.

"Perhaps the smoke from what we do will float over all of Europe," she said, her voice the same as when she was praying before. "And also to England. And the new world as well, new as it is. For no land will long survive without its tyrants. May it be a testament to all who breathe it that God wills us free."

They continued to burn one page at a time. Sometimes Cecelia called a name aloud when she supposed a page contained a certain person's words. Goris sat rigidly upright between them, staring out the window at the white smoke flying and scattering in the early morning wind, blowing downward into the city streets, upward and away in the direction of the North Sea, skipping and dancing like a kite.

Page by page they slowly fed the fire, Pieter waiting each time until Cecelia had dropped a sheet before following.

Suddenly Cecelia was a little girl back in the convent in East Friesia. She heard herself intoning words from the Latin funeral Mass. Her voice was steady and loud, but slow, saying a few words with each burning page. "Per dominum nostrum . . . Jesum Christum . . . filium tuum qui tecum . . . vivit et regnat . . . unitate Spiritus Sanctus . . . Deus per saecula saeculorum."

As she spoke she could tell from the corner of her eye that Pieter was watching her, listening to her, and wondering. "Some of it was beautiful," she said, as if Pieter were about to challenge her, continuing to burn the pages, not looking directly at him.

"Yes," he said. "Some of it *is* beautiful."

As she began to repeat the words, again in Latin, Pieter recited them in German, Goris joining them in Dutch, in perfect unison with both of them. "Through our Lord Jesus Christ, thy Son, who lives and reigns with you in the unity of the Holy Spirit, one God forever and ever."

"A finished story which has no ending," she said as they reached the last page which was the first. "We have reached the beginning. There is no ending," she said, as if to clarify what she had just said. Goris continued to sit between them, whimpering softly, making no effort to conceal the sound. "That was the error of Rome and Wittenburg. Of Geneva and Zurich. And almost us as well. To end the story. The end of a story can only be defended with violence. Nothing else is left."

Pieter sat now with his arms folded across his chest, watching with Goris as the smoke blended with the gathering clouds, the clouds accepting and embracing it like a vacuum. Cecelia continued to speak, softer now. "The tattered coat can never be possessed."

The wind had shifted and a slight gust down the chimney livened the coals, blowing a wisp of the white smoke, the very last of it, back into the room. Cecelia leaned into it and inhaled deeply. Goris and Pieter did the same, saying nothing, Pieter no longer sobbing. "Until we came together we knew the words," Cecelia continued. "Now we know the tune."

Chapter Seven

WITHOUT MOVING FROM the bench where they sat they heard the hoofbeats of what sounded to them like a legion of horsemen, approaching slowly and deliberately. They were quiet now, sitting as close to each other as they could get, sitting as one person. They did not move and did not speak again until there was a loud knocking, followed by a continuous rattling of the latch chain. Goris started for the stairs.

"No," Cecelia said, catching him by the hand, her voice calm and warm.

"We will let them in together.

"And together we will go with them."